TITANIC 2012

Dust Jacket Design: Alexander DeLarge
Typesetting and Design: Eric Blair
Printed in the United States of America

Cemetery Dance Publications
P.O. Box 943
Abingdon, MD 21009

TRUE FIRST EDITION
10 9 8 7 6 5 4 3 2 1

TITANIC 2012

BILL WALKER

CEMETERY DANCE PUBLICATIONS

Baltimore

❖ 1998 ❖

To
The Fifteen Hundred
and
James Cameron's Titanic
May both live long in our hearts and memories

Acknowledgments

I want to give special thanks to Alf Newsome, and everyone at Marine Art Posters in Hull, England, for kindly granting us the license to use *Titanic Poster No. 9* for the front cover, and thanks to Ronnie Mesriani, Susan Rooshanak, and Evan Mathis of Digital Room for their wonderful work and their patience with a neophyte.

Thanks to Tibor Szakaly for his exceptional rendering of the White Star Line burgee that graces the back of the dust jacket and all the Day/Date pages throughout.

Thanks to Harold Grey and International Typeface Corporation for customizing their Algerian font for the book's cover.

And thanks to Howard Rubin and Brian Dunn from Bauer Wines of Boston for all their expertise in matters of the grape.

Many thanks to Richard Chizmar of CD Publications for his early interest in the project and for his considerable leap of faith in going with a first novel. You're the tops, Rich.

Special thanks to Ed Kamuda of the Titanic Historical Society for giving permission to use a facsimile of the famous "On board" *Titanic* stationery for the Deluxe Lettered Edition. Ed, I really wish *I* could donate the $20 million. THS deserves it.

And last, but not least, I want to thank Elizabeth Klungness, first for encouraging me to expand my original short story to novel length, and then for all of her sage and incisive editorial guidance. Thanks, Elizabeth, for steering me clear of all the icebergs.

WEDNESDAY
MAY 2, 2012

1

The furor in the media had just died down when Solly's call came that rainy midweek day. I'd been hiding from the wolves of the fourth estate for nearly three weeks, holed up in my book-filled condo/prison in Charlestown, unable even to slip outside for a breath of fresh air without some cookie-cutter reporter, with a paint-by-numbers smile, sticking a microphone in my face and asking me the same tired question: "What was it like?"

As if the whole of my experience could be quantified in a sound bite.

Truth was I was avoiding everyone, even Julia and her earnest attempts to help me sort through the miasma of doubt and pain.

Sweet Julia.

We've been on-and-off again for the last five years. And I hadn't seen her for the better part of a year. I guess she thought now was as good a time as any to mend fences. Christ, if she only knew....

And what was worse, the book I'd promised my publisher, the one that was supposed to chronicle all I'd been through, lay like a beached whale on the shore of my imagination. I was standing at the bay window overlooking the harbor, watching the rain sluice down the glass, wondering if I would ever have the courage to write again, when my gaze shifted to the pile of audio mini-DVDs lying in a scattered heap on the teakwood coffee table.

My eyes filled with tears for the umpteenth time.

"I'm so sorry, Maddy," I groaned, knocking my forehead against the cool glass. "I'm so goddamned sorry."

"You have a call," the computer intoned in a quiet contralto, making me wince. Even the goddamned computer's voice reminded me of Madeleine.

"Who is it?" I asked, expecting to hear it was yet another call from the *Globe*. Hometown reporters were the worst, the most ravenous.

And then I remembered that I'd instructed the computer to screen all calls, allowing access to only a select few.

"The caller has an Identity Block in place. Shall I take a message?"

I sighed.

To hell with it. I had to rejoin the human race at some point, even if I felt as if I no longer belonged in it.

"Put it through," I said, making my way over to the sleek black Compaq Millennium sitting atop my writing desk. The monitor came to life and Solly Rubens' round face filled the screen. His saturnine looks were etched with concern, an expression that somehow looked ominous on him.

"Hey, Hughes, you okay? How are you holding up?"

The tiny "picture-in-picture" in the upper lefthand corner of the screen showed me what Solly was seeing, rendering his question moot.

I looked as if I'd taken the cook's tour of Hell: blue eyes—red-rimmed and puffy—surrounded by dark circles, sandy hair greasy and disheveled, three-day growth of a patchy red-flecked beard, and the same clothes I'd worn since Monday. I looked sixty-two, instead of forty-two. All in all, I presented a picture about as far as one could get from what *Boston* magazine had called: *"The World's Most Eligible Author."*

"How the hell do you think I'm holding up?" I said, staring back at Solly. His eyes blinked rapidly and I debated whether or not to instruct the Compaq to disconnect, when he spoke again.

"Shit, I'm sorry. I really put my foot in it, didn't I?" he said, trying to appear contrite. "Listen, I know we've never been the best of pals, but we had some good times back in school, didn't we? I mean, Christ, we've been through a hell of a lot since Harvard. You a hotshot writer. Me hittin' the big time. Shit, I can't believe it's been a year—"

"What do you want, Solly?"

His porcine eyes darted somewhere off-screen, then riveted onto mine.

"Ken and I thought you should get out of the house, maybe meet us at the Harvard Club. What do you say?"

"I don't want to talk about it."

"You *gotta* talk about it sometime," he said, his Brooklyn tenor rising in pitch. "You've been avoiding us for weeks, you look like crap, and everybody—and I mean *everybody's*—been trying to find out what the fuck happened out there. And what about Julia? You shutting *her* out? You treatin' her like shit, too?"

I resented him bringing her name up, only because I knew he was using her as leverage, and not out of any real concern for her feelings. Not that I was any better.

"She's none of your business, Solly. Leave her out of this."

"All right, I'm sorry. But you *know* I'm right. You gotta get on with your life, for Christ's sake. If you're not gonna do it for yourself, do it for Harlan."

I leaned forward, my nose practically touching the screen. "Where were *you* when Harlan needed the three of us? Huh? Where the hell were you when the fucking chips were down? Taking Karen to another New Broadway show?"

Solly's lips compressed into a thin angry line. "Okay, I deserved that. But Ken and I have a right to know what happened."

So, that was it. Like everyone else, they wanted to know the truth about Harlan's death—wanted to know all the gory details. Christ, they were no better than the goddamned muckrakers slinking around my front door. And why was it so important to Ken and Solly, anyway? Would it bring Harlan back? Would it bring *any* of them back? Why the hell couldn't they just leave me alone?

And then, all at once, the anger passed, as if someone had thrown a switch inside me. Suddenly, I wanted very badly to tell someone— anyone. And perhaps it was more than fitting to do it where it all began.

"All right," I said. "I'll meet you guys at the club, Friday night at six."

Solly cracked a grin, revealing crooked yellow teeth. "It'll do you good, Hughes, you'll see."

"Maybe.... But drinks and dinner are on you."

He chuckled.

"My pleasure. See you there."

The screen went dark, and I sat there for a long moment, wondering if I shouldn't blow them off. And then I realized that Harlan would *want* me to go. I doubted very much, however, once they heard the whole story, that it would be any pleasure for any of us....

◈　　◈　　◈

By five-thirty that Friday, when I left my condo, the rain had intensified, crashing down in a raging torrent all-too-familiar in the Northeast, the last gasp of the latest El Niño.

I picked up a cab at the corner stand, told the driver the address of the Harvard Club and settled back into the rayon plush of the mock leopard-skin seat covers.

"How do you wanna go?" he said, eyeing me in the rearview.

I thought about it for a moment. "Stay on this side of the river. We'll take Land Boulevard to Memorial drive and cross at the Harvard Bridge."

The driver nodded. "I tell you, bud, you made the right choice. Besides bein' more scenic, you don't get the congestion. I just took a fare down to Rowes Wharf through the fuckin' Artery...." He shook his head, his jaw working a piece of gum. "Man.... Those goddamned bastards who spent all that money puttin' that piece of crap underground forgot that people was movin' into the city at the rate of a hundred and twenty a day all during the time they was buildin' it. Now, it's as bad as it ever was, except you gets to look at tile walls and breath all that lovely exhaust, too. And if you have an accident? Forget it!" He shook his head and pulled the cab out onto Charlestown Avenue, heading for the Gilmore Bridge.

I leaned back in the seat and tried to order my thoughts, absently patting the leather briefcase that contained my mini-DVDs, along with the recorder. My story was only part of it. If Ken and Solly wanted to know what *really* happened, they would learn it the way I did.

From them....

The cab pulled up to the Harvard Club's brownstone edifice at 374 Commonwealth Avenue at precisely six p.m. I smiled. Harlan would have appreciated my punctuality. And when I entered the club—my senses taking in all the old familiar sights and smells: the dark mahogany paneling adorned with the framed portraits of past university presidents, plush red carpet, and leather-covered chairs permeated with the smell of expensive cigars—the sense that he was lurking somewhere about, in spirit at least, overwhelmed me.

I found Ken and Solly exactly where I expected to find them: in the front parlor seated at the round table overlooking the street. Unlike last time, the table was set with linen and silverware, the bone china painted with the Harvard crest. What struck me as odd was that Harlan's empty seat also had a place setting, as if they expected him to make a last minute appearance, laughing that it was all some cosmic joke. My anger returned, in spite of the fact that I knew the oversight was more the fault of the club than that of my friends.

Ken was the first to spot me, since Solly's back was turned. He flashed a weak smile and raised his glass of scotch in salute. I wondered how many drinks he'd had already.

Of the three of us, Ken Faust had aged the worst, the skin sagging on his long face, making him look like a sad old hound dog. Most would put it down to the pressures of turning a garage software business into a juggernaut rivaling Microsoft at a time when few would have thought it still possible. I knew the truth, however: the death of his young son from leukemia, and a marriage gone sour had eaten the heart out of him.

Ken nodded to Solly, who stood and turned, his meaty hand outstretched. I took it, feeling his warm flesh envelop mine in a viselike grip. He clapped me on the back. "Glad you could make it, Hughes. You clean up good, too."

His innocent reference to the fact that I'd showered, shaved and changed my clothes came out of his mouth sounding like an insult. I ignored it, taking my seat to the left of Harlan's chair, my back to the six-foot sash windows.

One couldn't blame Solly for his faults. He'd been crapped on in school, called all sorts of names, "kike" being the least of them. But he showed all those snooty WASPs a thing or two by making a killing on Wall Street during the crash of 2000. And after the SEC gave him a clean bill of health, he'd sent all his detractors "Get Well" cards each with a torn half of a hundred dollar bill in it. Some say he's still counting his profits.

As soon as I'd settled into my chair, a waiter appeared dressed in a red jacket festooned with brass buttons and gold braid. "Would you like something to drink, sir?"

I stared at him a moment then nodded to Solly. "Since my esteemed friend is paying for tonight's repast, I think we should have something fitting.... Chateau Lafite Rothschild, 1942."

The upward arch of the waiter's eyebrows was subtle, and he swiveled his gaze to the others, as if waiting for one of them to signal his approval or let him in on the joke.

Solly chuckled, shaking his head. "You always were a wine snob, Hughes." He nodded to the waiter. "Go ahead and bring it. Why not?"

Why not, indeed? It was the rarest vintage the club owned and cost about $10,000 a bottle. I thought Harlan deserved at least that much.

We waited in awkward silence until the waiter reappeared with a bottle on his silver tray, surrounded by three gleaming crystal goblets. He set it down on the table, pulled out a corkscrew and began the elaborate ritual of opening the seventy-year-old wine. Solly scowled, pulled out one of his ever-present Churchill cigars and lighted it, puffing away like an old steam locomotive. With his flaming red hair and the smoke spewing from his mouth, he resembled nothing so much as a fire-breathing dragon. From what I'd heard from others, it was an apt description of the man, as well as his business practices.

The waiter handed me the cork, and I waved it under my nostrils. I nodded for him to proceed and watched him pour a small portion into one of the goblets, which he then set in front of me. I picked it up by the stem and swirled the deep crimson burgundy, noting its strong legs, then brought it up to my face and inhaled deeply. The wine's nose was still full-bodied, piquant and fruity, with the characteristic cinnamon snap known to all the Rothschild reds. And even more important for a wine of this vintage: there was not even a hint of vinegar. She was an elegant old lady past her prime, but would drink well.

"Perfect," I said to the waiter. "That'll be all."

"Very good, sir," he replied, bowing slightly. He turned and left, and I picked up the bottle, feeling the pleasant heft of it.

"Normally, I would wait at least twenty minutes before drinking a wine of this quality," I said. "Under the circumstances, however, I think waiting would be an unpardonable sin."

I poured about three ounces into each goblet and handed them out. I then raised mine and said: "To Harlan Astor, friend and compatriot. May he finally find the peace he deserves."

"Hear, hear," Ken mumbled, taking a tentative sip.

Solly only nodded, swigging down the wine in a single gulp worth, by my estimation, at least eight hundred dollars.

Ken broke the uneasy silence that followed my impromptu toast. "What happened out there, Trev? The media's filled with all kinds of wild rumors."

"And you're not helpin' it any by clamming up," Solly cut in. "Some people are saying it's your fault, you being the only—"

"My fault?" I chuckled. "Now that's a good one."

I hadn't eaten all day and the wine was already making me lightheaded. I refilled my goblet and took another generous swallow, eager for the numbing euphoria it would bring.

"What about it, Hughes?" Solly said, annoyed.

I turned to him and met his gaze, then Ken's, who looked down almost immediately. "You sure you guys can spare the time?"

Both men remained silent, their guilty eyes the only indication that my barb had found its intended target.

I reached for my briefcase and placed it on the table in front of me, unsnapping the latches and throwing open the lid. I pulled out the mini-DVD recorder and the tiny three-inch disks, stacking them in a neat pile that emitted a golden glow in the soft lighting of the club.

All but one.

I could not bring myself to share Maddy's life with them. I left her DVD in the briefcase, which I placed flat on the floor at my feet.

"What's this?" Solly asked, waving his Churchill at my equipment.

"Ever since your call, Solly, I've been culling the interviews I conducted, dictating my part in all of this. I've been up for the last two days. I guess I should thank you."

"For what? Insomnia?" A wry grin spread across his face.

"For waking me up, for making me realize the story *needed* to be told.... And for keeping my publisher from taking out a contract on me."

Ken laughed, the wine finally loosening him up.

"Seriously, once you hear this, you'll both understand."

And wished to God you didn't, I added silently.

I reached over to the pile of mini-DVDs and picked up the one lying on top, placing it gently into the recorder. The drawer, sensing the weight of the disk, slid shut with a soft wheeze. The disk whirred silently, and a red light on the face of the machine began blinking, changing to a steady green.

It was ready. God only knew if *I* was.

Taking another sip of wine, I set down my goblet, pressed the "play" button, and settled back into the chair, listening as a stranger's voice—my voice—blared from the speakers:

"My mind says that nearly a year has passed, but to me it seems more like a lifetime...."

SATURDAY

JUNE 4, 2011

2

I hadn't planned on going to my twentieth reunion that Spring. I kept telling myself that it was a silly anachronistic practice, that I needed to look forward, not back, that I didn't give a damn.

But I did.

The real reason I wasn't going was that I felt I hadn't done anything of lasting value with my life, and that my classmates would look down on a man who wrote popular fiction for a living. And mysteries at that. So, when the alumni mailing arrived in February, I gave it a cursory glance and threw it out. It was Julia who plucked it from the trash that night and brought it into bed.

"You know," she said, running her long fingers down my arm, "if you weren't such a knucklehead, you'd admit that you're dying to go."

I kept my eyes on the manuscript pages I was working on. I was trying—and failing, thus far—to get my detective hero, Conrad Holm, out of a corner I'd painted him into.

"I have absolutely no desire to hang around with a bunch of fat middle-aged men reminiscing about the good old days. And that includes yours truly."

"You're not fat," she said, pinching my stomach.

"Hey, that hurt!"

"Sorry." The mischievous gleam in her hazel eyes belied her apology. "And being middle-aged isn't so bad."

"Thank you, Ms. Freud, for that cogent analysis."

"I'm Jungian. And what's so bad about a reunion, anyway? They're supposed to be fun. And they are. I went to mine."

"I remember. I also remember that I never heard the end of how fat so-and-so had become, and how many husbands such-and-such had gone through."

"Well...gossip is *half* the fun."

"Not to me," I said, striking yet another lame sentence.

"All right, What is it? What's really bothering you?"

"It's nothing. What's a synonym for obstreperous?"

"Knucklehead."

I sighed and put down the pages. "You're going to bug me until I tell you, is that it?"

She smiled her smug psychologist smile, leaving me no doubt. So, I sucked it up and told her.

And she laughed. It was completely natural and without rancor. "Good God, Trevor, you must be kidding! You've been on the bestseller list three times, once for almost six months. Everyone loves your books. You've got nothing to be ashamed of. Besides, I'll bet half those snobby bastards will want your autograph."

I shook my head.

"This is Harvard, Julia. I was supposed to be the best. We all were."

"You *are* the best."

"I think you're just a teensy bit biased."

"Why, because we sleep together? I mean, it's not as if we're married—"

"Let's not get into that again."

"I'm not," she said, rolling her eyes. "I'm just trying to tell you that you're selling yourself short."

"Am I?"

She sighed. "Yes. You are! So, you haven't written the 'Great American Novel' yet. So what? Most of them are pretentious crap, anyway. Your books have truth in them *and* they're fun to read. Besides, I was a fan of yours *before* we met. Or had you forgotten?"

Actually, until she'd said it, I had. We met four years ago at one of my book signings, her nordic beauty and slim athletic body an immediate attraction. I signed her copy of my new book and she'd hung around, standing off to the side, appraising me with that subtle enigmatic smile on her generous lips. I was hooked.

After the signing, we'd gone for coffee, and I was pleasantly surprised to discover she also had a brain. Ten years younger than me, she was completing a doctorate in Clinical Psychology at Radcliffe, and had fascinating opinions on everything. I remember we finished the night at her place, a cozy studio on Mt. Vernon Street, and there I received another pleasant surprise: her education had not inhibited her libido in the slightest.

Now, four years later, we spent three nights a week together and were very comfortable with each other. At least until the subject of marriage came up. As much as I cared for her, something held me back. Fear of commitment? Sure, that was a part of it. I'd been a bachelor far too long not to be a bit skittish. But I think I was also waiting for something more, some spark, some magic moment that would tell me this woman was the "right" woman.

It was a silly romantic notion, and something especially odd in a man, at least I thought so. And yet, it was a notion that had stayed with me my entire life. I guess the problem was that Julia was someone I was *too* comfortable with—a good friend, with whom I happened to have a sexual relationship. And while she was an exceedingly attractive and intelligent woman, I didn't *feel* that magic—I wasn't in love with her. And therein lay the rub, for Julia was madly in love with me.

I realized that I'd begun to daydream when her voice cut into my thoughts.

"...you hear me?"

"What? I'm sorry."

A look of mild annoyance flickered across her face.

"I said, I think you should reconsider."

"The reunion?"

"Yes."

"And I suppose *you* want to go."

She laughed again. "Oh, no. I wouldn't dream of cramping your style."

"And what style would that be?" I said, not a little amused.

"The carousing, the beer guzzling contests. That sort of thing."

"You know I don't drink beer anymore."

"Wine, then. Just think about it, okay?"

Resigned, I nodded my head and held out my hand. She placed the crumpled pamphlet in my palm and I gave it a quick read. I had to concede her point. A part of me *did* want to go, and the more I studied the scheduled activities and thought about seeing old friends, the more that part of me came to dominate the rest.

By nightfall, I'd resolved to go.

Four months later, I borrowed a friend's Mercedes SLK and drove over the Mass Avenue Bridge, through Kendall and Central Squares and on into Harvard Square. Things hadn't really changed all that much in twenty years. The buildings had a little more ivy and the bricks in the sidewalks a few more cracks, but it still had the old feel...and all the old smells.

I parked the car next to the ancient seventeenth-century cemetery with its tilting slate headstones and took a walk around. The news kiosk was still there, smack in the middle of the square, though it had been given a hideous new facelift as had the Red Line subway entrance; and the old man selling magazines and papers was now a different man decades younger. Seeing it all again made me smile nonetheless, sepia-tone images fraught with nostalgia flooding my mind. But it was the Wursthaus that brought back the most compelling images of all. It still squatted across the street from the Coop, dressed in its ugly mock-Tudor facade, looking for all the world like a blowzy bar maid out for a good time.

I recalled many a beery night spent there with Ken, Solly, and Harlan scoping out the babes when we should have been studying. Christ, twenty years...and a new century. It was staggering. And so were the prices on the menu posted outside the restaurant. Twenty bucks for a lousy burger! How could a student afford that? Shaking my head, I was turning to go, when I heard a gruff, familiar voice behind me.

"Hey, Hughes, I thought I'd find you here. You owe me a brewski!"

I spotted a stocky redheaded man dressed in a natty charcoal-gray four-button suit with a big grin plastered across his ruddy face, barreling toward me.

"Solly?" I said, my own grin widening to match his.

He grabbed me by the shoulders. "You're lookin' good, kid, real good. I read your last book, by the way. Great stuff!"

I suppressed a tiny smile, remembering Julia's admonishments.

"Thanks, Solly. And you're looking good, too!"

He gave me an incredulous look. "Get the fuck outta here. I've gained thirty pounds since the last time we saw each other. Eating too much crap like this," he said, indicating the Wursthaus.

"Have you seen Ken or Harlan?"

He chuckled. "Are you kidding? They asked me the same question about you. We're meeting up at the carnival. After that we're on the river cruise as personal guests of the president. You up for it?"

"I thought only VIPs got to do that."

"They do. But it helps when you endow a chair in Finance," he said, his grin turning sly. "Guess that makes me a VIP."

"You? Endowing a chair? After all the crap you went through?"

He shrugged. "What the hell. Holding a grudge never did anybody any good. And it's a great write-off. So, you wanna come, or what?"

Five hours later, after attending the carnival and the river cruise, and touring the campus to see how the old yard was faring, the four of us convened in the front parlor of the Harvard Club: Ken, Solly, me...and Harlan Astor.

Seeing him again after all these years brought back another rush of poignant memories. He still had the same boyish charm and rapier wit, and his face remained ascetically thin, the dark almost feminine eyes flashing as he spoke. He looked good, if a little pale.

As for how he'd managed out in the "real world," Solly had whispered to me during the carnival that Harlan had made his fortune in real estate, that he owned half of New York City and was busily negotiating for the remaining half. I knew Solly was exaggerating a bit, but it was gratifying to know that Harlan now carried his branch of the famous Astor name into the new century with its former wealth and luster restored.

The first hour we spent catching up, and after a while, when the conversation about business and family began to lag, Harlan began "The Game." It was something like Trivial Pursuit, only without the dice and cards, and each player had to try and come up with questions that would stump the others. It was an intellectual game played strictly for laughs. Still, we liked to make it a little interesting: whoever had the highest score got to choose who paid the bar bill. It was now my turn, and I was losing badly.

"What make was the gun Booth used to shoot Lincoln?" I said.

Harlan smiled at me as a parent would to a child. "A .44 caliber Derringer. You must be scraping the bottom, kiddo. That was too easy."

I shrugged. "I guess that's why I never win this thing."

"Leave off him, Astor," Solly said. "Let's see you come up with a better one. Your last two were pretty lame, too."

The crystal tumbler filled with Chivas Regal paused halfway to Harlan's lips, a devilish gleam shining out of his dark eyes. "Okay, then," he said, "here's a tough one. What's the greatest movie of all time?"

"For cryin' out loud, that's easy," Solly said. "*The Last Battalion.* Best war picture ever."

Harlan signaled the waiter for a refill and shook his head, a crooked smile creasing his face. "Good flick, Solly, but too dark for the masses."

"*Citizen Kane,*" Ken offered, taking a sip of his scotch. I noticed his hand shake and I looked away, embarrassed for him.

Solly groaned and rolled his eyes, placing his own glass on the waiter's silver tray.

"Another one, neat," he said.

Harlan turned to me, his eyes regaining that impish twinkle. "How about you, Trev. Got an opinion? You writer types always do."

I ignored the dig and swirled the runny slush that had once been my frozen strawberry margarita. "I don't know...*Gone With The Wind?*"

Harlan raised his glass in a mock salute. "Not bad, kiddo, but not by a long shot. You jerks give up?"

"Yeah, yeah, get on with it," Solly said, lighting his Churchill cigar, puffing steadily.

"James Cameron's *Titanic*—hands down."

"Harlan's right," Ken said. "I remember taking Margie to see it on our second date. We were both bawling like babies by the end. I think I must have seen it three—maybe four times."

The others nodded, remembering their own reactions to the film. As for me, my girlfriend at the time thought I was dangerously obsessed with it. I had the *Titanic* screensaver on my PC, I'd purchased the companion coffee table book, *two* copies of the movie poster, and multiple copies of various magazines detailing the behind-the-scenes aspect of the production. I'd even joined the Titanic Historical Society. I also realized that I hadn't thought of it in years. Funny how things can capture your imagination so completely for awhile, then fade away.

"Do any of you remember reading that Cameron actually considered rebuilding the ship?" Harlan asked.

Solly scowled. "Aw, come on, that's one of those stories the media likes to make up. Makes for good copy. Isn't that right, Trev?"

People assumed that if you wrote for a living, you must know all about the inner workings of the editorial departments of every magazine and newspaper. "Maybe, Solly," I said. "I don't know."

"It's true—at least partially," Harlan continued. "Among other ideas he ultimately rejected, Cameron briefly thought about having a bare-bones replica built at the Gdansk Shipyards in Poland. Would have cost about $25 million back then. The problem was time. He discovered it would take two and a half years to complete, and he didn't want to wait."

It was then I noticed Harlan's expression had changed, a dreamy look in his eyes. He leaned forward in his chair, as if it were taking every ounce of his will to stay in it.

"What are you driving at?" I asked, not a little curious.

The waiter returned with the fresh drinks, and Harlan took his and smiled.

Damn that smug look.

The others stared at him, caught up in the suspense.

Harlan chuckled. "You guys look as if someone were about to tell you you'd all gone broke." His expression changed again, turning serious. "Well, I've *done* it, boys...."

"Done *what*, for Christ's sake?" Solly cried.

"I've rebuilt the *Titanic*."

The words hung in the air for a long, awkward moment, and then the three of us burst out laughing.

"Oh, that's rich, Astor, really rich," Solly said, putting down his drink.

Harlan gazed down into his scotch, appearing to study the rainbow reflections dancing off the facets cut into the tumbler. "You guys think I'm kidding," he mumbled.

"Hell, yes," Ken said. "I lost count of all the pranks you pulled during school, not to mention those joke gifts you send us every Christmas. Besides, how the hell could you build that boat without the world knowing it? It's not exactly—"

"Normal?" Harlan said, cutting him off. "That's what you were going to say, wasn't it?" Anger had turned his face a mottled pink.

"No, Harlan, it wasn't," Ken said, shooting me a troubled look.

I felt things were getting out of hand, joke or not. "Come on, you guys, it's not worth arguing over."

Harlan turned his laser beam gaze toward me. "Not worth it? You forget my great-grandfather died on that ship. As well as fifteen hundred others."

"So, what's your point?" Solly said, all humor gone.

For a moment, Harlan was without a response, then his characteristic swagger returned. "My point, is that it's almost the hundredth anniversary of the sinking. I want to honor them."

"By rebuilding the worst symbol of twentieth century excess?" I said.

"Right down to the last rivet."

I shook my head.

"Wait a minute. Money aside, I still can't see how you could do that without someone finding out. You'd have to have a construction crew of at least ten thousand on a project like that."

"Fifteen thousand," Harlan replied, icy calm.

"That's a lot of flapping gums, Astor," Solly added, knocking back another gulp of whiskey.

"I promised each worker a $5,000 bonus if the ship reached completion in utter secrecy. In Poland that's still a bloody fortune."

Ken's jaw dropped. "Jesus Christ! That's—"

"About seventy-five million.... Plus another six hundred million for the ship. It's going to be perfect."

"You've lost it, pal." Solly said, shaking his head. "Really lost it."

"Well, then, I guess you won't want a berth on its maiden voyage next April."

"You got that right. It's a goddamn waste." He chuckled drily. "You gonna bring your own iceberg, too?"

Solly's laugh grated on me, as did his obvious contempt for our friend. Maybe he was jealous that someone would blow that kind of money on a personal whim—a fantasy. Then again, maybe he had a point. Maybe Harlan was losing it. Still—

"How about the rest of you?" Harlan asked, his narrowed eyes darting from one man to the next.

Ken shrugged and stared into his drink. "I can't think that far ahead, Harlan. You know me."

"Trev?"

I hesitated only a moment before speaking.

"I think it's probably the nuttiest thing you've ever done, Harlan, but if you'll have me, I'd like to go. Maybe I'll write an article about it."

Harlan's face split into the widest grin I'd ever seen him make. "Somehow, I knew I could count on *you*, Trev."

Solly drained his drink and stood up. "Well, it was grand seeing you guys, but I gotta go. Promised Karen, we'd catch a Broadway show tonight. You coming, Faust?"

Ken shot a nervous glance at Harlan, then stood up. "Yeah, great to see you guys."

A moment later the two of them were gone, and I saw a visible change come over Harlan. He sagged in his chair, suddenly looking far older than his forty-two years.

"Have I lost it, Trev?" he asked, staring at his hands. I noticed they were fists, the knuckles white.

"I loved that film as much as you, maybe more. But you have to admit, it's an awful lot of money to spend on a dream."

Harlan met my eyes then, his own like two smoldering embers. "Is it...? I've often wondered about that, kiddo. Maybe, when all is said and done, all we've really got are our dreams...."

We went our separate ways a few minutes later, and during the drive back to Charlestown I kept running Harlan's last statement through my mind. While I could sense the excitement in him over this incredible project of his, I couldn't shake the feeling that somewhere underneath it all, something was troubling him. I tried to call him, but his cell phone was turned off.

When I got home, there was a message from my agent and one from Julia. Suddenly, I very much wanted to talk to her to get her take on what Harlan had told us. She picked up the phone in her office on the first ring, unusual for her.

"This is Dr. Magnusson, may I help you?"

"Hi, your secretary leave early?"

"I wish," she said, her voice tight with exhaustion. "She called in sick this morning and the phone's been ringing off the hook. Half my patients are down with some kind of bug."

"I'm sorry, I guess the last thing you want to hear is how the reunion went."

"Actually, I could use some distraction. How about dinner? My place."

"How about we order in?"

"Even better. See you at seven?"

Julia lived on the summit of Beacon Hill, and from her apartment situated atop a two hundred-year-old Federalist town house, nestled in the shadow of the State House, her view was nothing short of breathtaking. At night, the lights twinkling from Cambridge and Back Bay looked like an electric tapestry.

I arrived at 7:05 bearing two large bags filled with several cartons of food from her favorite Chinese restaurant down on Charles Street. She'd already prepared the table with plates, silverware, an open bottle of Chardonnay, and a pair of flickering candles.

"God, that smells good," she said, kissing me and grabbing one of the food bags out of my arms.

I followed her to the table and the two of us began dishing out the egg rolls, Kung Pao Chicken and steamed rice.

"Almost as good as you look," I said.

She laughed. "Flattery will get you everywhere. Especially today."

"That bad?"

"You don't want to know. The one appointment that did show, came only long enough to tell me she was quitting therapy. Said she was getting married and didn't need me anymore." She took a bite of the spicy chicken dish and rolled her eyes in ecstacy. "Damn this is good. How'd you know I was thinking about this?"

"I know you all-too-well, Ms. Freud."

"You do at that.... So how is Harvard faring?"

Without going into excruciating detail, I filled her in on my day. Even with the "Reader's Digest" version I was giving her, I could tell she was only paying partial attention, her thoughts no doubt consumed with her own problems. But when I got to Harlan's fantastic revelation, her whole demeanor changed.

"He actually said he was rebuilding the *Titanic*?" she asked, giving me a dubious look.

I nodded, grabbing for the carton of rice. "Wild, huh?"

"I think your friend is in need of serious therapy."

I laughed. "That's what the rest of us thought, too. But when I saw the look in his eyes, I could tell he was serious—more than that, actually. Haunted would be a better word."

Julia frowned.

"Has Harlan ever talked like this before?"

"What do you mean?" I asked.

"Has he ever demonstrated behavior like this in the past."

"Do you mean, has he ever blurted out something grandiose, and not followed through with it?"

She shook her head. "No, you said he was 'haunted,' that's what I mean."

"About what?"

"Did he appear to be reacting to unseen stimuli, like hearing voices?"

I put down my fork.

"Julia, what are you talking about?"

"I think your friend might be borderline delusional."

"Whoa," I said, holding up my hands. "Time out. Just because my friend, as you put it—my obscenely rich friend, I might add—says he's rebuilding the *Titanic*, you're ready to pack him off to the loony bin?"

"I didn't say that. But you have to admit it's a pretty wacky thing to do."

"Yes, I said that, but—"

"And just to honor his great-grandfather and the others who died?" She shook her head and picked up her glass of wine. "If he's not having a psychotic break, he's got the most colossal ego I've ever seen, not to mention that it's a colossal waste of money, too. My God, he could do so much more good just giving it to his favorite charity."

"Well, he's not. And that's *his* business," I said. "The money thing really bothers you, doesn't it?"

"Yes, it does. What the hell is he going to do with it, anyway? Charter rides?"

I smiled at the thought. "That wouldn't be a half-bad idea. I can think of a few million people who would jump at the chance. Hell, *I'd* like to. In fact, he's invited me on its maiden voyage."

I saw a look flash across her face, a mixture of shock and anger, and something else I couldn't quite read. "And what did you tell him?"

"That I'd love to write an article about it."

"Hey, why not a whole damn book?" Her voice had taken on an edge. "You can call it, *Ego Trip*."

"What the hell is with you?"

She threw down her napkin and stood up. "I don't know, maybe I'm superstitious. Maybe I don't think anything good can come out of rebuilding *that* ship! Maybe I don't want you to go, all right?"

She started to cry, large tears, like pearls, welling out of her eyes. I went to her and took her in my arms, feeling her body trembling against mine. If the situation weren't so ludicrous, I would have been aroused.

"Hey, hey, it's okay, it's not the end of the world," I said, caressing her hair. "It's just a stupid boat ride. Besides, I don't even know if I'm going to have the time. I've still got to finish the new book, or its sayonara, Conrad Holm, hello unemployment."

"But you *want* to go, you just said you did."

"I said, I'd *like* to. That doesn't mean I will."

She pulled away and looked me in the eye, her manner calmer. "I'm sorry.... I guess I'm just a little too much on edge lately. My practice is going to hell and this just pushed me over."

"What's really bothering you, Julia? It can't be just about me going on that ship."

"But it is, Trev. You forget, I saw that movie, too. I *know* the power it has. It makes people want to be a part of that world. And that's not normal."

I shrugged.

"Maybe, not. But look at the world we live in. Was that one so bad?"

"In some ways, yes, some ways, no. The point is it's gone, and all the money in the world isn't going to bring it back."

Looking into her face at that moment, I suddenly realized the true nature of her fear. "You're afraid I'm going to meet someone, that I'm going to have some kind of shipboard fling, aren't you?"

She remained silent, staring out the bay window.

"Oh, come on, Julia," I said, laughing. "You know me better than that."

"Do I?"

I took her by the shoulders and turned her to face me.

"You know I care for you.... Very much."

"I know...." Her eyes were like two bottomless lakes, cold and unfathomable. "But do you *love* me, Trev?"

I felt a rush of anger. I'd been neatly boxed into a corner by a professional, and I resented it. Yet, I knew she was hurting, and wanted to ease her pain. The issue, however, was a thorny one. If I simply told her what she wanted to hear, I would be no better than some low-rent Lothario eager to bed a woman at any price. And I knew I couldn't live with that. The other choice—living without her—was just as bad. I'd grown comfortable being with her. Then again, perhaps being comfortable was the problem. We'd become complacent, at least *I* had.

When I didn't answer right away, I saw her withdraw into herself, like a light dimming in a room, deepening the shadows.

"I think you should leave, Trevor," she said, in a voice barely above a whisper.

"Julia...."

"Just go, dammit, just go."

No longer angry, and feeling adrift, I picked up my jacket off the couch and headed for the door, turning to look at her one last time. She'd gone to the window, and now stood there staring out at the lights, her back to me, arms clasped around her chest, as if to keep herself from flying apart.

"I'll call you," I said.

"Please...don't."

I left.

Outside, the air was chilly, and I saw thick dark nimbostratus clouds hovering on the western horizon. It would be raining by morning.

I turned up my collar and began the long hike down the hill, my mind churning. I'd been a heel, or at least I felt like one. And yet, lying to her about my feelings was never an option. Maybe, in time, she would come to appreciate that. Right now, however, I knew we were finished.

I picked up a cab in front of the Red Line station and during the ride home, kept remembering what she'd said about *Titanic's* vanished world, how no amount of money could ever bring it back. And while I harbored my own doubts about Harlan and his crazy dream, I also knew—without a shred of doubt—that I wanted to be on that great ship when she sailed.

MONDAY

FEBRUARY 6, 2012

3

The news of Harlan's extravagance finally broke that morning. I was revising the middle section of my book for what seemed to be the hundredth time, trying to tighten up the pace, when my monitor suddenly went blank.

"You have a news alert," the computer said.

Annoyed, I reached for the "Escape" key. "Not now, Millie."

Although it was considered to be unnecessary, I'd given the computer a name, a diminutive of its model designation: Millennium. I think the Artificial Intelligence program—a gift from Ken—responded better as a result, then again, maybe it was just my over-fertile imagination.

Millie's voice took on a note of urgency. *"The news item concerns subject: Harlan Astor."*

That changed everything. "Put it on."

I sat back in my ergonomic chair, adjusting it for passive viewing, while Millie brought up CNN. *"Engaging surround sound,"* she said.

The Lucas/THS speakers mounted on the walls behind me crackled to life and the picture on the monitor faded up on the CNN newsroom. The anchor, a young Asian beauty I'd never seen before, was reading off the TelePrompTer with studied irony.

"...We now have confirmation that the rumors swirling around New York real estate tycoon, Harlan Astor, are true. For the past two and a half years, the semi-reclusive Astor has been involved in a secret construction project in Poland, known—until now—as 'Project X.'

"Sources in that country have revealed the incredible news that Astor has been employing a vast army of fifteen thousand laborers to rebuild the *Titanic*, the grandest ocean liner of all time, which tragically sank one hundred years ago, taking over fifteen hundred lives. Our correspondent, Rita Newton, is standing by in Gdansk with more of the story."

The scene shifted to a stark industrial landscape: soot-streaked brick buildings, steel gantries, smokestacks, and cranes jutting skyward, all of which combined with the gray featureless sky overhead to make the young blonde reporter, standing in the glare of the lights clutching her microphone, appear pale and washed out—like a ghost.

My pulse was pounding and my hands ached from clenching the armrests of the chair. The reporter began speaking, her voice and demeanor earnest.

"This is the Gdansk Shipyards, one of the largest and busiest centers for shipbuilding in the world. Behind me, shrouded in its own building to shield it from the prying eyes of the world, lies the nearly completed hull of what many are calling: Astor's Folly.

"At a cost of nearly six hundred million dollars, Harlan Astor has spared no expense to recreate the *Titanic*, the most famous ship ever built. And while there have been numerous others since that have been larger, none has ever achieved the magical allure of that ill-fated vessel.

"No pictures have been made available, nor were our cameras allowed anywhere near the forbidding black hangar where the great ship lies in its slipway awaiting launch.

"As for more details, a spokesman from Mr. Astor's European headquarters in London informed us that a press conference would be convened on March twenty-first, six weeks from today. Until then, no further information would be forthcoming. And that leaves the world asking, why? Why would a man spend a fortune to rebuild a tragic symbol of a century many would like to forget? For an answer, we will all have to wait. This is Rita Newton, CNN, Gdansk, Poland."

I rose from my chair and went into the kitchen where I pulled out an IBC Root beer. "Millie, turn to NBC."

"Executing...."

The channel switched to Brian Williams's report and gave pretty much the same coverage, though the correspondent in Gdansk seemed angrier, more contemptuous of Harlan's audacity, as well as his silence.

The other networks were evenly divided in their coverage between those who saw Harlan as insane and wasteful and those who saw his rebuilding the *Titanic* as a metaphor for redemption. And just like CNN, none of them had any footage of the ship. I smiled. Like P. T. Barnum at his peak, good old Harlan was going to make them wait. By the time of his March twenty-first press conference, the press and the rest of the world would be at fever pitch.

I overrode Millie's voice commands and switched off the news manually, going back to my book. Harlan called half an hour later.

He looked haggard on the screen, but his face glowed with an inner light, as if he were plugged into a wall socket. Either that, or he was on something.

"Hey, Trev! How are you? Bet you forgot all about me, huh?"

"Out of sight, out of mind," I replied, grinning.

"You always were a lousy liar, kiddo. That's why your books are so damned good. They're honest."

"Well at least you saved yourself some money," I said, referring to the now-forfeited secrecy bonus.

Harlan's smile widened. "Yeah, there's that, too."

"What happened?"

"Oh, hell, some riveter got drunk on too much vodka and blabbed to a roomful of people. Somebody with an itch for network money heard him and put it out on the wire. What can you do?" He shrugged again. "I never expected to pay it, anyway. All I wanted to do was buy myself some peace and quiet for as long as possible."

"How does she look?"

Harlan leaned closer to the screen, his eyes glittering. "I can't wait for you to see her, Trev. She's everything she was...." He turned and nodded to someone offscreen, then turned back toward me. "We're launching her at the end of March—"

"Yeah, I heard about the press conference. Ought to be a real party."

"I'm counting on it, kiddo. This time the old girl's going to get a proper christening! And I want you here with me when she goes. What do you say?"

"Christ, Harlan, I'm in the midst of revising my book. I've got a deadline breathing down my neck and a publisher who's ready to blow a gasket if they're late to press. I can't just drop everything."

He gave me a sly look.

"You seriously expect me to believe you'd miss the biggest story in twenty years?"

He knew me too well.

I sighed, glancing out my window toward Old Ironsides where she lay permanently moored. She was a great ship, but her days of greatness were past. Now, another ship would get a *second* chance. And I wanted to be a part of it.

"What's it going to be, Trev?"

I turned back from the window and fixed him with what I thought was a sober expression.

"All right. I'll talk to my agent. Maybe, if he doesn't think I'm out of my mind, he'll talk to my publisher. Maybe he can convince those pirates this cockamamie idea of yours would make a helluva book."

"Now, you're talking. Hey, listen, I've got to go, but I'll see you here on the twenty-first!"

The screen went blank and I collapsed back in my chair, breathless. The sonofabitch had really done it. He'd gone and rebuilt the grand old tub. And in a little less than two months I would be seeing her in all her glory.

It took me a solid hour to calm down, and I used the time to formulate a pitch. It had to be more than just a recounting of Harlan's dream, it had to touch people. A moment later, I had it. Excited now, I called my agent, Marty Scott, and told him I would meet him at Tavern on the Green at noon the next day.

Like any good agent, Marty was curious; and he could sense the excitement in my voice. "You've got something, don't you?" he asked, his voice betraying his own excitement.

"Yes, I've got something. And you'll just have to wait until I see you, okay?"

Marty shook his bald head and smiled ruefully. "I never could stand to be in suspense. How the hell I ended up selling mystery and suspense novels, I'll never know." He chuckled. "What the hell, it's a living. See you tomorrow."

I couldn't stay in that night, so I opted for a prime rib dinner at Durgin Park. I loved that old Boston landmark with its communal tables, simple food prepared to perfection, and its no-nonsense waitresses, none of whom were under forty.

The only sour note in the evening occurred when I thought I'd spotted Julia with another man at a table across the room. It turned out to be someone else, but I couldn't help feeling a twinge of jealousy. Hell, she had every right to find someone else, and yet my wounded ego persisted in gnawing at my heart. It took all of my will not to pull out my cell phone right then and call her. I still had her programmed into my speed dial.

I finished the evening in a little neighborhood dive down the street from my condo. The crowd was always full of regulars, friendly blue-collar types who had enough common sense to leave you alone if they sensed you needed to be. I sat in a booth near the jukebox and drank enough cheap sangria to put me into a deep, dreamless sleep later that night.

In the morning, I had the barest of hangovers, which I soon dispelled with a hot shower, a homemade cappuccino, and two fat extra-strength Tylenols.

Throwing on a chambray shirt and some khaki Dockers I hadn't worn in a while, I grabbed my leather A-2 jacket off the coat stand and left. I caught the ten o'clock shuttle at Logan and made it to Tavern on the Green by 11:45.

41

Marty, as usual, was already seated at his customary corner table, yakking away on his cell phone, an ice-cold martini sitting in front of him, dripping with condensation. He spotted me weaving through the tables and waved. When I drew closer, I caught the tail end of his conversation. It was pure Marty.

"...and I don't give a flying fuck if he is the CEO. He doesn't know jack-shit about publishing. He and his board forked over two hundred million for the company and now they're dicking around trying to run it," he paused and winked at me, then motioned for me to sit down. I complied, gratified to see that he'd ordered me an iced tea instead of my customary wine cooler. After last night's binge, I had no desire for anything alcoholic for awhile. I took a sip and waited while he continued.

"...that's right. I told Fran she was going to get her royalties *on time* for a change, and I always come through for my clients. I don't lie to them. And I sure as hell won't be lied to. Is that understood? Okay, call me later, we'll talk turkey." He clicked the phone closed, placed it on the table and clapped me on the shoulder. "How's it hanging, Trevor?"

"Fine, Marty. Trouble in paradise?" I said, nodding toward his phone.

He shot me an "are you crazy" look, dismissing my question with a casual flick of his hand. "Just some lousy pencil pusher," he said. "Most of the time they do their jobs. But sometimes they screw up—big time. And that's when I gotta play hard ball. You watch, I'll have her check by the end of the week." He aimed a finger pistol at me and fired, then took a sip of his martini. The glass looked like a toy in his hand.

I've always thanked the gods for the day that Marty Scott agreed to be my agent. Like all of them, he couldn't make miracles, he couldn't sell the unsaleable. But he was a tireless advocate for his clients; and someone you didn't want to cross.

"So what's the big deal?" Marty asked, "or did you just want a free lunch?"

I suppressed a smile. It was kind of fun to be the one with the information, for a change. "Have you watched the news the last couple of days?"

Marty shrugged. "Unless it has something to do with my clients, I don't pay much attention. What about it?"

I told him about Harlan and the *Titanic*, and true-to-form, Marty watched me with a deadpan, almost apathetic expression on his jowly face.

"So, what's the hook?" he asked when I'd finished.

I leaned forward. "Harlan's invited me on the maiden voyage. What I'm proposing is to write a sort of shipboard diary, sprinkled with interviews of a random group of passengers, get their take on *why* they wanted to sail on the new *Titanic*. Was it the movie, the ship herself, or something else? We can serialize it for the Net, as well as make it a full-blown book eventually."

I waited, my palms damp with nervous sweat, while Marty swallowed the rest of his martini. "I don't see it."

"Come on, Marty, it's a natural. Every April they show Cameron's film on TV. It's a goddamned tradition, just like the *Wizard of Oz* and *It's a Wonderful Life*. I even hear they're considering a major theatrical re-release to capitalize on the one hundredth anniversary of the sinking. Harlan's voyage will be the capper, and I'll be right there."

I sat back and swirled my iced tea. Marty still had the same inscrutable expression on his face, and I was beginning to feel the first tendrils of doubt creeping into my thoughts. Maybe the idea *was* a clinker, and I was just too swept up in it—too blind to see it.

My fears eased when I spotted the twinkle in his eyes, the clear indication he was seeing dollars signs. "You know, kid," he said, signaling the bartender for another round, "you just might have something there. Hell, I always liked that movie, myself."

Too nervous to eat, I stayed and watched while he picked up his phone and called the editor-in-Chief of Mannheim Books, a personal friend.

"Ronnie, how ya doing...? Great, can't complain.... Hey, that's great to hear.... Say, listen, Ronnie, my client, Trevor Hughes, just clued me into a great idea for a book you're gonna love...."

Mannheim Books bought the pitch on the spot with a promise of a high six-figure advance. Not only did they want to do the book, they loved the idea of putting it out on the web, a sort of "Dispatches at Sea" sort of thing. Marty was especially effusive for the remainder of our lunch date, even picking up the tab. That surprised me. I loved the guy, but he was a notorious tightwad.

I spent the next six weeks polishing the final draft of *Conrad's Revenge* and personally dropped it off on Marty's desk on the nineteenth of March. Harlan's press conference was two days away.

Everywhere I went, people were talking about the *Titanic*, wondering what my friend was going to say, or if it was all some grand joke. I remembered what Ken had said back at our reunion about Harlan's penchant for wacky presents.

Every Christmas, without fail, Harlan mailed each of us a gift. Always useless in the extreme, it was nevertheless a gift guaranteed to bring a smile to the recipient's lips. They were always different, and almost always expensive, like the time he sent me a shiny new set of Black & Decker electric hedge clippers, along with a card that said: *Bring 'em to their knees, kiddo!* He knew I lived in a condo, with nary a hedge in sight, yet he'd sent it, anyway. That was Harlan. I ended up mounting it to the wall of my study with a blow-up of his card. It was both my inspiration and my taskmaster.

These thoughts ran through my mind all the way over on the Concorde, which streaked over the North Atlantic at twice the speed of sound. Lulled by the quiet thrum of the engines, I gazed out the tiny window at the great expanse of blue water below. Not so much ice as there used to be. Still, I couldn't help thinking that somewhere two miles below that smooth, cerulean surface lay the rusting hulk of the original *Titanic*, swathed in eternal darkness, unaware of her impending rebirth.

The sleek SST landed in Warsaw at 8:00 p.m. local time on March twentieth. Rain gouted from out of low roiling clouds, and I said a little prayer that tomorrow's events would have more favorable weather. I tried not to think of it as some kind of omen, as if my friend had somehow offended the gods.

After I'd cleared customs I took a cab to the train station and boarded an express for the coast. Assuming there were no downed trees from the storm or any other unforseen mishaps so common to the Polish rail system, I would be in Gdansk by midnight.

Harlan had thought of everything. Aside from the pricey ticket on the Concorde, an extravagance I fully enjoyed, he'd gotten me a private compartment on the train. I liked European trains, for though they were as sleek and as modern as any in the United States or Japan, they still retained the quaint modular design, whereby each compartment opened onto the platform. As for the compartment itself, it boasted standard seating for four (both seat backs folded down to beds), two fold-down writing desks the size of postage stamps, each replete with a data port, and a well-stocked mini-bar. Unfortunately, the only beverages offered were thimble-sized bottles of mediocre vodka and cans of a local soft drink, the name of which I could not decipher. In any event, it was cozy and didn't smell too bad.

Sitting down, I propped my feet up on the swing-out footstool, sighing when the soft plush of the seat molded itself around me. That, and the clackety-clack of the wheels, began to calm me. I fell into a fitful sleep, awakening only twice, once for the conductor asking for my ticket, and once to use the tiny closet of a bathroom. Aside from that, no one bothered me during the entire four-hour trip.

A frigid wind was howling in off the Baltic when my train pulled into the Gdansk station. I'd somehow managed a cramped shower and changed my clothes. The train hissed to a stop, and I grabbed my bag, stepping out onto the platform. This late in the evening, the station was deserted, with only a handful of maintenance workers on-hand to greet me and my fellow passengers. Even after my long nap, I was still tired, and my neck ached, as if twisted by some sadistic chiropractor. All I wanted was to get the hell out of there and grab a cab to the hotel. As usual, Harlan had me covered.

Outside the station, I dashed for the line of cabs idling at the curb. Suddenly, I heard a horn blast directly behind me. Startled, I turned and spotted Harlan standing up through the sunroof of a stretch Mercedes limo, grinning from ear to ear. He looked thinner than he had on my computer screen six weeks before; and there were dark circles under his eyes, but if anything, his enthusiasm had only increased.

Leaping out of the Mercedes, he encircled me in a bear hug. "It's great to see you, Trev. Come on, there's a lot to tell."

While the limo wound its way through the city's darkened and desolate streets, Harlan filled me in on the upcoming schedule of events.

"The press conference tomorrow is scheduled for 11:00 a.m. Immediately after that, we'll move out to the hangar for the christening and the launch. You'll never guess who I've got to wield the champagne."

I shrugged.

"Kate Winslet."

"You're kidding. I heard she was in the middle of shooting a picture in South Africa."

"She is. But I paid off the producers, the cast and crew, and gave them all a week off. Besides, only a great woman like Kate should christen a ship like this."

He laughed, and I had to admit I envied him his ability to think so big—and his wherewithal to bring it off.

"The press know anything, yet?"

Harlan cracked a sly grin. "Those sonsabitches are practically foaming at the mouth, if you can believe that."

"Oh, I believe it. After I hit the bestseller that third time, my publisher had me on a signing tour for two months straight. And everywhere I went those bozos asked the same dumb questions...." I shook my head remembering the inanity of it all.

After a ride of twenty minutes, the limo pulled up in front of our hotel, a soot-blackened pile of rock that looked as if it had been through a war. Then I realized that it had been through at least two.

Inside, the grand old dowager had retained much of her dignity and appointments, enough to make it seem as if I were in one of New York's or London's lesser hostelries.

After I checked in, we had coffee in the restaurant. I was surprised to see that the place was busy at one o'clock in the morning. Harlan read my mind.

"Most of these people don't eat dinner until ten o'clock at night, some even later," he said, shaking his head. "I don't know why they don't all end up with reflux disease. Then again, I'll bet they sell lots of TUMS here."

He laughed and ran a hand through his hair. I noticed it was a lot grayer than at our reunion nine months before.

"I've been meaning to ask you something, Harlan."

"Shoot."

"You told us back in June why you wanted to do this. But, now that you're almost there, has it been worth it?"

He stared back into my eyes with the kind of look that I can only describe as prophetic. Not in the way most people use that word, but as in a prophet of the Old Testament: intense, with a touch of divine madness. And it thrilled me and scared the hell out of me all at once.

"Ask me that after tomorrow," he said, picking up his espresso. "Then again, you won't." The crazed look was gone, replaced by one of tired satisfaction. "She's really a beaut, kiddo, a real knockout."

"You have many passengers booked?"

"About two hundred, thus far," he said, staring into his cup. "I've decided to limit the passenger list to five hundred for this trip. I'm sure I'll have the rest by sailing day. As it is, I've had to turn a lot away...."

"Why?" I asked, puzzled. "Surely not the money?"

Harlan shook his head, a distracted look creeping into his eyes. "No, money isn't the main criterion on this voyage. I'm just being very selective."

After a few more minutes of small talk, we called it an evening and I took the elevator up to my suite. Again, Harlan had surprised me by booking me into the Presidential Suite: A master bedroom, a sprawling sitting room and a smaller, but no less extravagant bedroom adjoining. In all, over two-thousand square feet of bygone opulence. I was mortified.

"Jesus Christ, Harlan," I said to myself, "you're spending it as if someone were about to take it all away from you." I shook my head and went to the phone, intent on calling down to the front desk to request a room change. It rang before I reached it.

"Hello?"

"How do you like it, kiddo?"

"Harlan, it's wonderful. I feel like the Sultan of Brunei, but I don't *need* it. It's way too expensive."

He laughed. "You're saying that to a guy who just spent six-hundred million on a boat?"

"My point exactly."

"I've got news for you, Trev. My accountants are begging me to form a foundation. It's piling up faster than I can spend it. So, relax and enjoy it. You're only here for one night, anyway."

I sighed. It was no use arguing over it, plus I was beat. And the wide king-size bed did look inviting. "All right. You win."

"Naturally," he said, chuckling. "Oh, I've sent up a little room service, too. Enjoy."

"Harlan, I'm not hungry—"

He hung up before I could say anymore. Two seconds later there was a knock on the door.

"Yeah?"

"Room service," came the heavily-accented reply.

I opened the door to find a uniformed waitress standing behind a cart draped with white linen and silverware. In the center was a champagne bucket, the top of the bottle poking out. Next to the bucket was a plate filled with caviar-topped canapés. Never one to refuse a gift (*it obviously didn't do any good, anyway*), I waved the young lady in. She pushed the cart into the middle of the room and presented me with a bill. I signed it, then reached for the bottle.

I almost dropped it when I saw the label: Dom Perignon *1912*. A note was attached, and I opened it.

Just a little something to get you in the mood. It's great having you here. Harlan.

It was then I noticed that the waitress was still there, and there were *two* champagne flutes on the cart. I turned to let her know everything was fine and nearly dropped the bottle again.

She was stark naked, and breathtaking.

"I am to please," she said, her voice low and throaty, eyes downcast.

I swallowed, my throat having gone dry. "Uhh, excuse me?"

"I am to please," she repeated, a flush spreading across her ample chest and up her long, slender neck.

"I got that. Did Mr. Astor arrange this little *tête-à-tête?*"

She bit her pouty lips. "I do not—"

I shook my head. "Sorry. Did Mr. Astor *pay* you?" I rubbed my thumb and forefinger together.

The girl's face lit up. "Yes! Big dollars!"

"Oh, brother," I said, placing the champagne back in the bucket. I started to reach for the phone to call Harlan. During our initial conversation on the ride to the hotel, I'd mentioned that Julia and I were no longer an item. He'd obviously arranged this—in his own inimitable way—to help me get her out of my system, but when I neared the phone, the girl became hysterical.

"Please, do not call police!" She trembled with terror, and I felt sorry for her. To tell the truth, she was damn attractive. But I was dog tired and not really in the mood.

"All right, you can stay. But no hanky-panky."

"No panky-hanky?"

"No."

She shrugged her shoulders and began putting on her scattered clothes. On impulse, I decided to throw caution to the wind and opened the champagne, pouring a glass for each of us. It was marvelous, somehow both drier and more subtle than I would have expected from a century-old bottle of champagne.

Between the two of us, we polished it off in twenty minutes, and then we went to bed—me in the master bedroom, her in the other. An hour later, I awakened, feeling her slide into the bed, her smooth cool skin tingling my backside. A moment later she kissed my neck and reached for me.

I didn't refuse her.

The next morning, I awoke to the sun streaming in through the floor to ceiling windows. My bedmate was gone, as were the remnants of the champagne and caviar. For a fleeting moment I wondered if I'd dreamed the whole affair. Then I saw the condom's empty foil wrapper lying on the floor, and I caught a whiff of her perfume on the pillow next to mine.

Lavender. A curious scent for one so young.

Smiling, I glanced at the clock.

9:45.

In a little over two hours, I would be seeing the ship for the first time. A thrill ran through me while I showered and dressed in the one good suit I'd brought. Harlan had wanted us all to look our best for the press. *All the better for them to pillory us*, I thought.

Downstairs, I asked the desk clerk to ring up Harlan's suite. "Mr. Astor has already left, sir. However, he asked me to inform you that his car is at your disposal."

"Thank you," I said, shaking my head in wonderment. If this kept up, I would be spoiled rotten. Too nervous to eat, I left the hotel and found the Mercedes limo waiting at the curb, a cloud of exhaust pluming in the morning chill.

The uniformed chauffeur, a young Pole with a Cheshire cat grin on his face, leaped out of the driver's seat and held open the rear door. I climbed in, and a moment later the limo sped away.

The closer we drew to the Gdansk Shipyards, the heavier the traffic became. The chauffeur, still grinning, expertly threaded the ungainly vehicle through the streets. We finally reached the gates at 10:30. The guard, a stolid type with a shaved head and a face full of freckles, eyed the papers proffered by the chauffeur and waved us through.

I knew that late in the last century, when Poland had still been communist, the shipyards were state-owned. One giant operation. Now, years after going private, the yards were home to dozens of firms, all of whom competed. Harlan had told me that the actual areas where the ships were built—the slipways—were shared and had to be reserved far ahead of time. "I had to pull a lot of strings to get this project ahead of all the others," he'd said. I could only imagine it meant more money, no doubt greasing the palms of those who had learned well the art of capitalistic graft.

The Mercedes traveled the central road toward the water, and I noticed dozens of news vans lining both sides, their satellite dishes pointing skyward on the end of long telescoping poles. Aside from CNN, all five U.S. networks were represented, plus news organizations from nearly every major country in the world.

We came to the end of the street and turned the corner. More news vans were parked in front of the main building at the far end, and a crowd—perhaps numbering in the hundreds—choked the road, milling about in a state of nervous excitement. There appeared to be a lot of families, too, possibly those of the workers.

It was then I saw that nearly the entire length of the street on the quayside was dominated by the black hangar enshrouding the ship. Set out about fifty feet into the harbor, and reached by a wide concrete jetty, it looked even more monolithic than it had from the shots I'd seen on Millie's monitor.

Smooth atramentous walls towered over three hundred and seventy-five feet in the air and stretched a thousand feet in length—enough room for both the ship and the overhead gantry needed to construct it. When we drove past, I saw that the entire structure was mounted on rails, no doubt motorized, allowing it to unsheathe the ship for launching. A large flag-draped reviewing stand stood right up against it. The flags were the red-and-white swallow-tailed burgees of the now-defunct White Star Line.

The chauffeur pulled up in front of the main building and held open the door for me. I climbed out, my eyes searching for Harlan.

"Mr. Hughes?"

I turned and saw a young bespeckled woman walking toward me, her hand outstretched. "Hi, I'm Trina McCloskey, Mr. Astor's assistant," she said, gripping my hand firmly.

While not unattractive, she was dressed severely in a dark pinstriped suit, her hair pulled back from a lean triangular face. Her eyes, a light brown, appeared to be magnified through the thick lenses of her wire-rimmed glasses.

"Nice to meet you, Trina. Where's Harlan?"

She indicated that we should start walking and led me toward the building. "He's in a meeting with the owners of the yard. Settling accounts."

I smiled, imagining the wide-eyed gleam in those men's eyes while they watched Harlan sign a six-hundred-million dollar check. Of course, I knew things were not done that way, but it made for an amusing image.

"Where are we going?"

"Mr. Astor requested that I take you into the press room. We're almost ready to start."

The "press room" turned out to be a cavernous chamber painted an institutional green, and looked to be a hastily-converted cafeteria. Row after row of folding chairs had been set up facing a raised platform at the far end of the room. In the center of the platform stood a podium bathed in television lights and bristling with a profusion of microphones. Minicams on tripods lined both sides of the room and filled the back, and every one of the folding chairs held a member of the world's press, chattering away with his or her neighbor. The noise level gave me an instant headache.

"Can I get you anything?" Trina yelled, her voice shrill.

"How about some aspirin?"

She smiled for the first time, revealing a mouthful of capped teeth. "I know what you mean."

"I'll be fine, that is if I can find a place to sit." I said.

"Your seat is at the extreme right," she said, pointing to the makeshift stage and the row of chairs lined up behind the podium. No doubt these were reserved for the VIPs accompanying Harlan.

"If that's okay, I think I'll wait for Harlan." I said, nodding to the reporters. I had no intention of being the first on the dais and have all those newshounds staring at me.

Trina seemed to understand. She returned my nod and then left the room. I found a place near the back wall behind one of the camera crews and waited. Five minutes later, the doors opened up and Harlan marched in, Trina at his elbow, followed by a retinue of about a dozen people. I suspected they were the owners of the yard and others of Harlan's staff. I followed them onto the dais and took my seat where Trina had indicated. Harlan took his place behind the podium, a self-satisfied smile curling his lips.

I reached into my pocket and turned on my mini-DVD recorder. I'd debated all morning as to whether or not to bring it, finally deciding that it was far more accurate than my sometimes spotty memory. The microphone, a wireless affair disguised as a pen, sat sticking out of my front pocket.

The noise level in the room had exploded when Harlan entered and now began to subside, the reporters eager for their story. Harlan bent down to the forest of microphones.

"Ladies and gentlemen of the press, I want to thank all of you for coming. Rather than make a statement now, I am going to reserve my personal remarks for the christening ceremony. I will, however, entertain your questions."

A swarthy reporter with a mustache raised his hand.

Harlan pointed to the man. "Yes, sir."

The man stood and consulted a small pad held in his pudgy hands. "Pierre Emile, *La Monde*. Mr. Astor, the people of my country would like to know...why it is you have done this?"

Harlan turned toward me, our eyes making contact. He nodded knowingly, as if to say, "I see what you mean."

"You get right to the point, don't you?" Harlan said to the reporter.

The room erupted into laughter.

The conference lasted for half an hour, adjourning when Trina received word that Kate Winslet's limousine had arrived. Harlan led the way out of the room and the reporters followed. I caught up with him when he neared the entrance. "You enjoy your little surprise last night?" he asked, feigning a nonchalance I knew he didn't feel.

"I'm not telling. And where the hell did you get that champagne, anyway?"

He shot me a conspiratorial wink and said, "Moët et Chandon have kept a case from every vintage year since 1895. I bought the one from 1912. We're using one of the bottles for the christening."

I had to laugh. It was a typical Harlan Astor touch. God only knew how much money he'd parted with to persuade that prestigious winery to part with that year's case.

Outside the building, I was startled to see that the entire street fronting the black hangar was now completely filled with spectators. Several helicopters circled overhead, cameras mounted to their noses, their blades chopping through the air with the usual *whock-whock* sound.

When the crowd spotted Harlan, they cheered en masse, a happy lusty sound of those who'd completed a job well done. No doubt they'd also heard my friend had paid his bill in full.

We started down the wide steps and the crowd parted in front of us, like a scene from an old Cecil B. DeMille epic. Voices yelled endearments, and hands reached out to Harlan, seeming to caress him when he passed. I realized then that I'd misjudged these people. He'd seduced them with his dream, as surely as he'd seduced me.

Farther down the road, we met Kate Winslet's limousine, the chauffeur and bodyguards keeping the crowd at bay with baleful glares and intimidating size. One of the bodyguards opened the rear door and the winsome actress alighted, the sun striking her strawberry-blonde locks, making them glow as if aflame. She caught sight of Harlan and threw her arms around him. The crowd cheered again.

"Harlan, love, you look absolutely smashing," she said.

"So do you, Kate," he replied.

She laughed, her blue eyes sparkling.

"And you're a bleeding liar. I'm as fat as a dray horse."

At Harlan's request, she'd dressed for the occasion in a replica of the purple and white boarding dress from the film, the wide purple hat perfectly accenting the lines of her face. And while she was now a mature woman of thirty-seven, she was far from fat.

Harlan turned and said, "Kate, I'd like you to meet my friend, Trevor Hughes."

Her eyes widened. "Good Lord, the mystery writer?"

I felt myself blush.

"Guilty as charged," I replied, taking her proffered hand. Her skin felt cool and silken.

"I bloody love your books! I've read every one."

To say I was flattered would do a disservice to her compliment. I was, as the cliché goes, speechless.

"We'd better get this show on the road," Harlan said, breaking the spell. "Kate has to catch a plane."

Moving again, we stepped onto the concrete jetty and made our way to the reviewing stand. The crowd pushed forward, wanting to follow, but were held back by a cordon of armed police.

The reviewing stand, while large and accommodating to the dozens of dignitaries crowded onto it, nevertheless looked insignificant compared to the hangar, like a wart on a giant. Guards on the platform ushered the dignitaries and me to one side, allowing the crowd and the cameras to get an unimpeded view of Harlan and Kate Winslet. I saw that my friend now had a microphone in his hand, and when he spoke, his voice boomed out of the two speaker towers on either side of the platform.

"One hundred years ago, when my ancestor, John Jacob Astor IV set sail aboard the original *Titanic*, he had no idea what fate had in store for him and the 2200 others on board. They were of an age when nature and fate were presumed to be forces subservient to Man, and they learned of their folly in the most horrific of ways. And yet, my ancestor, and the others who died aboard that grand vessel, showed the world that the Spirit of Man was greater than all his works combined, and their sacrifice was the greatest of all legacies to come out of that harrowing moment in time.

"Now, we are at the dawn of a new age, an age that frightens many with its rapid changes and dizzying complexities, an age where once again we must demonstrate to the world that the Spirit of Man will not be daunted.

"Many have questioned my sanity. Many have questioned why I have spent such a vast fortune rebuilding this, the greatest and most tragic of all ships. I say to all those who would condemn me that they are a part of why our culture is poised on the brink of moral bankruptcy. And I say to you now that I have done this to honor those who died on her a century ago and to offer the world a new symbol of our spiritual rebirth....

"Ladies and gentlemen, I give you the spirit of a new age.... Ladies and gentlemen, I give you...*TITANIC!*"

A rumbling began under our feet, and at first I feared that an earthquake had begun. Then I realized that the hangar was moving, sliding back on its bed of rails. A hush had fallen on the crowd and thousands of eyes watched while the great black mass moved back farther and farther, picking up momentum.

The gantry appeared, foot after foot of crisscrossed steel girders. Suddenly, the leading edge of the hangar passed the reviewing stand and the bow of the ship stood revealed. Seconds later, I saw the word "Titanic" spelled out in giant twelve-inch yellow letters.

The crowd roared.

I moved back against the railing of the reviewing stand, craning my neck. The first funnel appeared, black smoke belching from it. Someone had fired the boilers. A minute later, the second funnel emerged...then the third, and finally the fourth. They looked like giant guardsmen marching in perfect single file. Five minutes later, the entire ship stood revealed in the late morning sun, its fresh paint gleaming.

Before the *Titanic* could be launched, the hangar shell had to be removed. When the hangar stopped moving, two Sikorsky skycranes moved into position, hooked up their cables and flew off toward another part of the yard, the hangar shell suspended between them. In any other situation, the sight would have been awesome. As it was, it could not compete with the magnificence that was the new *Titanic*.

With the sounds of the Sikorskys fading in the distance, Harlan helped Kate up the steps on the scaffolding leading to the bow. I had to hand it to her, she carried it off it like the trooper she was, climbing up those rickety-looking steel steps with aplomb in that tight, confining dress.

Someone tapped me on the shoulder just then, and I turned to find Trina at my side. She handed me a bottle of the 1912 Dom Perignon sheathed in a plastic mesh to prevent injury from flying glass.

"Mr. Astor has requested that you join him for the christening."

"Me?"

I suddenly felt as if the world's eyes were on me. In fact, they were. She nodded and disappeared into the crowd of dignitaries. Swallowing my stage fright, I gripped the bottle, holding it like a wide receiver running for the goal line, and moved toward the steel steps. I have to admit to a mild fear of heights. They make my knees feel as if they're going to buckle. So, I kept my eyes on Harlan and Kate while I climbed.

"How does it feel to have a front row seat, kiddo?" Harlan whispered, taking the bottle from me.

"Like I'm in a fishbowl," I said.

He grinned and attached the bottle to the harness at the end of a long rope. I looked upward and saw that it was tied off somewhere about twenty feet in front of us. The bow itself stood a little farther out. One good shove and the champagne bottle would slam right against the peak.

With the bottle secured, Harlan tugged on the rope, testing it, then handed the bottle to Kate. She swung it back and forth a few times, and looked at him questioningly. He nodded, extending the microphone to her.

"In the name of King Charles III, and by the grace of God, I christen thee...R.M.S. Titanic! May God bless her and all who sail on her...."

She reared back and let the bottle fly. It swung on its short arc shattering against the bow peak with a resounding pop. Champagne sprayed back on us and Kate shrieked with laughter, yanking off her hat and spinning it into the air.

Like gunshots, explosive bolts holding the ship in place began firing all along its keel, and a split-second later, the giant piston of the hydraulic launch trigger pushed forward. With a deep groan, the giant vessel slipped backward into the water on rails slathered with over fifteen tons of grease, giant chains attached to stanchions on the slipway pulling taut to check its momentum.

Cheering, the crowd surged along the quay, keeping pace.

Sixty seconds later, she floated in the harbor, free of her drydock and ready for her historic voyage. Her tri-tone whistle blew, and from everywhere in the yard, steam whistles answered, saluting her birth, while half a dozen tugboats pulled alongside in preparation for her escort out of the harbor.

Tendrils of steam escaped from narrow pipes fitted alongside the first three funnels, and then black smoke belched out in a great gout from the mouths of the funnels themselves, a sign that the mammoth reciprocating engines had started. A look to the stern confirmed it: the triple screws churned up the water, now brown with silt.

On deck, resplendent in their new White Star uniforms, the crew saluted and waved. According to Harlan, they would now take a short shakedown cruise, then head to Southampton for provisioning: he wanted the passengers to see her for the first time at the place from which she originally sailed.

Harlan left to escort Kate to the airport, but most of the crowd remained behind for perhaps another half an hour. I couldn't leave, either; *Titanic* held me in her thrall. I watched in awe while the tugs guided her toward the mouth of the harbor, a lump caught in my throat. My friend had made his dream come true.

And soon, in ways I could never imagine, he would make mine....

TUESDAY
APRIL 10, 2012

4

I set foot on the reborn *Titanic* one hundred years to the day her namesake first sailed. After the christening, I returned to Boston and spent the next week and a half making sure my publisher was happy with the revisions to *Conrad's Revenge*, conferring with Marty and my newly-assigned editor at Mannheim Books about the *Titanic* project, and trying to relax.

I finally gave up and left four days early, taking those few extra days to explore the English countryside before making my way to Southampton. I'd also tried to reach Harlan in the interim, but he'd proven to be frustratingly incommunicado.

Now, here I was, standing on the quayside, clutching my carryall and watching the most awe-inspiring sight of my life: the *Titanic* being readied for her maiden voyage.

Held fast to the docks by hawsers as thick as a man's arm, she dwarfed the buildings around her, funnels rising to nearly one hundred and fifty feet in the air—a reincarnated jewel sparkling in the sun. Anticipation and excitement crackled in the early spring chill, and I could read it in the faces of everyone I saw.

And people were everywhere.

Hundreds, maybe thousands, milled around or stood staring at the magnificent ship, their eyes wide with wonder; White Star crewmen, proud in their new uniforms, directed the loading of luggage and cargo, their voices shouting above the din; well-wishers hugged family members, eyes filled with tears, last-minute farewells whispered into anxious ears; and passengers streamed into the belly of the ship through the three different gangways for First, Second, and Third Classes.

It gave me a curious sense of *déjà vu*; the sight bore a remarkable resemblance to the boarding scene from Cameron's film, which I'd seen perhaps a dozen times. The only things that broke the illusion were the occasional anachronism: a jet plane streaking overhead, sleek ultra-modern cars parked by the quay, and news crews, their bright camera lights scattered about like tiny novas.

Jostled from behind by a crewman carrying his duffle bag slung over his shoulder, I strode toward the First Class gangway. Reached by a winding flight of stairs, the gangway stood suspended fifty feet from the ground. Again, my fear of heights gripped me when I stepped onto the narrow gangway, feeling it sway under the tramping of dozens of pairs of feet. A man nudged me from behind.

"Move along, there's a good lad," he said. His precise British accent startled me into movement.

I kept my eyes glued to the B-deck hatchway, and marched across as fast as the traffic allowed, breathing a small sigh of relief when I reached it. A White Star crewman, his peaked cap set at jaunty angle, addressed me as I came abreast of him. "Your name, sir?" he said, looking down at his clipboard. I noticed that it was made of solid hardwood, possibly mahogany, and fitted with polished brass fittings. Old, yet new.

"Trevor Hughes," I replied.

The crewman scanned the list through steel-rimmed bifocals, his lips pursed. "Ahh, yes, Mr. Hughes. Starboard side. Suite B-57/59."

Harlan had done it again. I'd been given P.O.S.H. accommodations: Port Out/Starboard Home. At least it was home for me. Smiling, I thanked the crewman and stepped onto B-deck, my soft-soled shoes squeaking on the teakwood decking.

One thing I'd noticed was that more than a few people were dressed in period clothing, making me feel like one of those anachronisms. I'd thought of doing so myself, but could not work up the nerve, fearing I would be the only one. I should have guessed that more than a few would succumb to the temptation, this being the greatest and most expensive re-enactment in history.

A middle-aged man dressed in tweeds and a starched collar so tall that it resembled a neck-brace, passed me with a smile and a tip of his derby hat, and I was altogether glad that I'd opted for modern comfort.

My suite, B-57/59, while not one of the "millionaire suites," one of which I subsequently discovered right next door, was nevertheless a study in opulence: a tasteful mixture of Empire and Old Dutch styles, the suite was paneled in a dark walnut-stained mahogany accented with polished brass wall sconces and fittings.

The walls above the wainscoting were covered in a richly brocaded green silk, echoed in the divan and two Biedermeier chairs. The bed, a four-poster style with fluted columns topped by a wooden canopy, was nestled into the corner just to the left of the stout paneled front door. I tested the mattress, my hand sinking into its down-filled softness. Definitely not for those with bad backs, I mused.

Turning back into the room, I noticed a framed black-and-white photo of an Edwardian couple affixed to the back of the door. The legend underneath identified them as the suite's original 1912 occupants: Arthur Larned Ryerson, Sr., and his wife, Emily. Apparently, for them, the voyage had been a sad one from the outset. The Ryersons, along with three of their children, were returning to the States for the funeral of their eldest son, Arthur, Jr., recently killed in an automobile accident. Ryerson, a homely silver-haired man in his early sixties, appeared stiff and formal, while his elegant wife stared into the camera with haunted eyes.

The portrait was a compelling and poignant touch, giving me a feeling of close connection to the past, and making me wonder what became of Emily and the children in the wake of the tragedy. According to the printed legend, Arthur, Sr.—like so many other men of his class—had not survived.

I resumed my exploration of the suite. A quick look into the other bedroom revealed a mirror image of my room with the bathroom shared between them. There was even another smaller room, B-61, accessed through an adjoining door, that would have accommodated my servant, if I'd had one. It seemed a waste to have all of this to myself.

Back in B-59, I threw my carryall onto the bed and began unpacking, eager to go on deck to witness the departure. When I opened the closet to hang my suits, I was surprised to find a set of tails, circa 1912, replete with brushed beaver top hat, opera cloak and all the accessories, including a set of pearl stud cufflinks and what appeared to be solid gold collar studs. A note written on cream-colored paper stuck halfway out of the breast pocket. I pulled it out and opened it. It was a reproduction of the original *Titanic* stationery. At the top of the sheet in the left-hand corner was the White Star Line's red and white burgee, and to the right were the words: *On board R.M.S. "Titanic."* Underneath that was a blank line for the month and the numerals 201, with the last number of the year left blank. The note itself had been written in black ink with a fountain pen, and it took me a moment to recognize the shaky scrawl as Harlan's.

If you are going to dine with "the better half" you'd better dress the part. See you in the First Class Dining Saloon at eight. Harlan.

And though the handwriting disturbed me, I couldn't help smiling at his allusion to Billy Zane's infamous line from the film. The *Titanic's* tri-tone whistle blew and I checked my watch.

Almost noon. Sailing time.

Grabbing my DVD recorder off the writing desk, I hurried from the stateroom, taking the stairs up to the Boat deck. Passengers clogged the rails, waving and shouting hysterically. Somewhere out on the quay a mid-size brass band struck up "Oh, You Beautiful Doll," and the crowd on the dock cheered back. Crewmen scurried about untying the hawsers from the cleats on the forecastle and poop deck and heaving them onto the quay, where dockworkers set about coiling the thick hemp ropes.

I moved to the starboard side and spotted four stout tugboats already alongside, ready to assist the *Titanic* out of the harbor. The tugs blew their whistles simultaneously and the *Titanic* answered with a blast of her own.

And then she began to move.

The cheering of the crowds, both on and off the ship, reached a crescendo. I returned to the port side, finding a space at the railing next to a middle-aged woman. She smiled at me and I nodded back, totally comprehending her nonverbal message. Yes, it was grand to be here.

A helicopter shot by, prompting me to glance upward. There were a dozen or more circling overhead, their Wescam-mounted video cameras ogling us like voyeurs. There were more cameras on the quay, both amateur and professional, recording our departure from every conceivable angle. In a way, I was a camera, of sorts, too. It would be my memories, coupled with those whom I captured on DVD who would paint the most vivid picture of this voyage. I wondered who would be my first interviewee and how I should choose him or her. Should I walk up cold, or get to know them first? It was something to which I'd only given the vaguest of thought and it bothered me. I'd never done nonfiction before, at least none that had involved this kind of technique. Library research was a different animal. Here I became a part of the story.

It took the better part of thirty minutes for the ship to clear The Solent. But once she hit the English Channel, her engines opened up and I felt the surge of power. I fully intended to explore the ship from bow to stern, but I had the entire voyage for that. Right now I was suddenly eager to visit the wheelhouse.

I found the Captain and his first officer standing on the starboard bridge wing, conferring. I was struck by his remarkable resemblance to Captain E. J. Smith: the regal bearing, the snow white beard. I'm sure this was deliberate, that Harlan had chosen the man both for the resemblance and presumably for his seamanship. I was more than a little curious about where and how he'd come to *Titanic*.

The tone of their conversation changed when they noticed me standing a few feet from them. The Captain said something to his first officer, who nodded and moved off. He then turned to me.

"May I help you, sir?" the Captain asked. His tone was affable, if a little remote.

"I'm sorry to bother you, Captain, but once we got underway, I couldn't resist coming up here. I hope it's all right."

His face creased in a warm paternal smile. "Of course. She's a beautiful ship. She should be explored."

"How fast are we going, by the way?"

He turned his weathered face to the wind, blue eyes squinting into the sun. "About eighteen knots. Would you like to see the wheelhouse?"

"Try and stop me," I replied.

The sense of *déjà vu* overwhelmed me again when we entered the wheelhouse. I'd seen it so many times in the film I could picture it in my sleep: the main telemotor and the auxiliary wheel, the commutator, and the intercom system, so primitive, yet so elegant.

The Captain watched me examining every artifact, then turned to the crewman behind the wheel. "Mr. Harper, let our guest take the wheel."

I suddenly felt like a kid again, like the time my grandfather had arranged for me to drive a train in the yard where he once worked. This, however, was far different. I grasped the wheel in my hands and watched the ocean through the bank of windows fronting the wheelhouse.

I was on top of the world.

"You're that writer friend of Mr. Astor's, aren't you?" the Captain asked.

"Yes, though sometimes I wonder if I shouldn't get a real job."

The Captain nodded, staring out the window a moment, my humor lost on him. I could tell that something was on his mind, something that bothered him. "Is anything wrong, Captain," I asked.

He turned back to me. "I was wondering," he said, hesitating a moment, "if you'd like to hear an old man's story?"

I smiled. My first interviewee had found me.

Returning the wheel to the crewman he'd called Harper, I pulled out my DVD recorder and placed it on a nearby ledge. "Do you mind if I use this?" I asked.

"Not at all."

"Just state your name for the record," I said.

He nodded, and I reached over and pressed "record."

5

Interview with Captain Earl Pierce
Location: Wheelhouse

Captain Pierce hesitated a moment, his eyes darting from the recorder back to me. "Is it on?" he asked.

I sensed that it might be intimidating him and reached for it. "Yes, but if you're uncomfortable—"

"No, no, leave it on. It just reminded me of my old life for a moment. What should I say?"

"Anything you want. Your name, age, that sort of thing."

The Captain nodded, taking a moment to gather his thoughts. "...My name is Earl Garrett Pierce, I'm sixty-two years old, and I remember as clear as a bell the day my life started going downhill....

"I was an advertising executive at one of the top agencies in New York, started in the mail room when I was twenty-five. God, it was exciting back then. All the old taboos were fading, people were willing to take chances, and I loved every minute of it. I got my break through a fluke. I'd been working on house accounts at home in my spare time, working up dummy campaigns. I was waiting for my big chance, never realizing it was about to ambush me." Pierce chuckled. "You see, somehow one of those dummy campaigns that I'd brought into work got mixed up with the mail. I've often suspected my cohort in the mail room of taking matters into his own hands. To make a long story short, it ended up on the desk of one of the partners, who read it and called me in. I thought my career was over." Captain Pierce smiled wistfully.

"He liked it, didn't he?" I prompted.

"He loved it, thought it was the freshest idea he'd seen in ages."

"What happened next?"

Pierce looked out over the ocean, then turned back to face me. "I was promoted to Junior Account executive and given the account, over the objections of the Senior Account Supervisor. She was one of those ball-buster types, had clawed her way up, and resented a young college-boy upstart waltzing in and dazzling the boss. She did everything she could to sabotage me. Christ, she even had the nerve to go to my clients behind my back and accuse me of stealing my colleagues' ideas. But my patron saw through it, and gave her an ultimatum: fly straight, or she was out. She tried to get along with me, but she knew it was all over for her. She was gone within a year. By that time, I'd proven my mettle, as my boss liked to call it, by not only increasing the sales of the accounts I'd handled, but by bringing in new ones, as well.

"Those first years saw phenomenal growth and I grew with it, helping to branch the agency out into different arenas."

He paused a moment and I took the opportunity to gently nudge him back on course. "You said you remembered the day your life started going downhill. What did you mean by that?"

Pierce sighed, took off the dark-navy-blue cap with its bullion embroidered White Star Line cockade, and wiped his brow with a folded handkerchief. "It all began in 2003. I'd been with the agency for almost thirty years, was a full partner and pulled down a salary of over a million and a half annually. And suddenly...I didn't want to do it anymore. I began spending more and more time sailing my forty-foot ketch. Sailing was my saving grace, you see. Spent all my spare time on that boat, and it kept me from succumbing to the madness that the business had become. Creativity was dead. All they wanted was to follow someone else's trend, rather than set them. My wife, Bette, finally made me see the light and I cashed out.

"Being a partner has its advantages, the main one being stock in the company. We might not have been half the company we used to be, but we were worth ten times as much as when I started. With my share in hand, Bette and I took our boat around the world. The trouble began when we got back...."

Pierce fell silent, and I resisted the urge to prompt him again, sensing he needed the moment to gather himself.

"Bette had cancer, you see, had known for months. It was something the doctors had told her was inoperable, nothing they could do. I was livid that she'd kept it from me. Felt betrayed. I told her, 'What good is a marriage if we don't tell each other the good *and* the bad?' She looked at me for the longest time, not saying anything except with those sky-blue eyes of hers, and then she said, 'Because I knew you would want to leave no stone unturned, and I couldn't bear the thought of your fighting so hard, only to lose.'"

Captain Pierce put his fist up to his mouth, tears welling in his eyes. "Excuse me," he said, wiping his eyes. "I'm sorry."

"That's all right, sir. Would you like to stop?"

He shook his head.

"No, I need to tell this."

I nodded for him to continue at his own pace.

"Of course, she was right, which only made me all the more angry. And yet, I loved her for it...her courage.... She died six months later, quietly and with little pain. I thanked God for that much, at least. And when I came home from the funeral, I suddenly realized that I no longer knew how to be alone. I went to bars and struck up conversations with whomever sat next to me. At first these people were charmed, and then began to avoid me. I suppose I was lousy company in the long run. Soon, I stopped using the loneliness as an excuse and drank in earnest. The house began to deteriorate, my boat sat in its slip rotting...."

"How did you—"

"—end up here?" Pierce said, anticipating my question. "After five years of steady drinking, I'd nearly hit bottom. Most of my friends, who weren't too numerous to begin with after Bette's death, deserted me. I was a very sloppy drunk, you see, couldn't keep from telling the truth about people, pointing out their faults." Pierced laughed without a trace of humor. "As if *I* were without sin.

"The crisis point came one night in August last year. I'd been on a bender for five days straight, ran out of booze and tore my house apart, screaming at the top of my lungs. I finally passed out, at least that's what they told me at the hospital, where I woke up shaking from the DTs and without a clear thought in my head, except that I wanted a drink.

"It didn't even register when the doctor, a young fellow who reminded me of myself, told me that my liver was shot and that I was too old to be worth the expense of a transplant. He told me in no uncertain terms that I was living on borrowed time and that any more alcohol and I would be dead. I looked into his mercenary eyes and asked him for a tall glass of grain alcohol, the kind they keep under lock and key and about 190 proof. 'That ought to do it,' I told him.

"He looked nonplused, to say the least, mumbled something about rehab and left me alone. It was then I received my little epiphany. The man in the bed next to mine told me about Harlan Astor and the *Titanic*. I thought he must be worse off than me, that he must be raving, but his eyes were clear and his hand on my arm was steady and firm. I asked him, "How come I've never heard about this before?' and he smiled, 'Because Mr. Astor wants only special people to know and has the money to make sure people keep quiet.'

"Well, I didn't think I was so special, and I told him so. He just laughed and then reached into his bedside table, pulled out a business card, and handed it to me. All it had was the telephone number and the phrase: *For the voyage of your dreams* printed on it. I still thought it was damn strange, stranger still because they had a rerun of *Titanic* on TV that night.

"Bette and I always loved that film. I guess, maybe because we saw a little of ourselves in those two lovers. After it was over, I fell asleep, and when I woke up the next morning, my roommate was gone. I never found out who he was."

"Is he on the ship?" I asked.

Pierce shook his head. "No, not that I've been able to ascertain.

But after I dried out, I called the number on the business card and an hour later was picked up at the hospital door by a large black limousine. Inside the car was none other than Harlan Astor himself. As soon as he saw me and heard that I'd been a sailor, he offered me the captaincy of *Titanic*. To say the least, I was floored, still not quite believing my good fortune, but he flew me to Gdansk and showed me that it was indeed real, as was the offer."

"And here you are."

"And here I am."

"Forgive me, Captain, but there's something I don't quite understand." I paused and he nodded for me to continue. "How is it you were able to get licensed to captain this ship? A forty-foot ketch is not the *Titanic*."

"No, it isn't," he said. "The first officer is fully-licensed. And I suppose he is the legal captain, insofar as piloting the ship is concerned. Even still, I've learned a great deal in the last few months."

"Does this give you the same thrill that advertising once did?"

"You're very perceptive. And the answer is: yes. I can't imagine doing anything else."

"Well, Captain, here's to a long and lustrous career."

He looked at me then, his expression ineffably sad.

"I'm afraid that will not be the case, young man, for along with my damaged liver, I have developed acute aortic stenosis. The doctors have given me less than three months.... You'll excuse me, now, but I must make my rounds."

Stunned, I watched him stride from the wheelhouse erect and proud, and I waited until he'd disappeared before reaching for the recorder and pressing "Sto—

FRIDAY

MAY 4, 2012

6

Solly shook his head sadly, watching while I pulled the disk from the DVD recorder and replaced it into its plastic jewel box. "So, this poor sonofabitch gets his dream job handed to him on a platter, and he's got three months to live?"

I didn't say anything, remembering both the sadness and the joy in Captain Pierce's eyes.

"Jeez, what a lousy break. What happened next?"

"All you'd gotten from Harlan up to then was his note, right?" Ken asked.

"Right. It was my plan after the Captain's interview to file a dispatch in the radio room and then go down to his stateroom and talk. But I got sidetracked."

Solly's eyebrows shot up.

"Yeah, how so?"

I yawned, then glanced at my watch. "The club's closing in half an hour. What do you say we call it a night?"

"Come on, Hughes, you can't just leave us hanging like this," Solly said.

Ken picked up my briefcase, which I'd forgotten to latch, and the lid fell open. The contents spilled out.

"Sorry, Trev," he said, bending down. He picked up a DVD, his eyes innocently scanning the label. "Who's Madeleine?"

I took it from him, avoiding his eyes. "She's not important," I said, regretting my tone of voice and the words as soon as I'd uttered them.

A sly grin spread across Solly's face. "Oh, I bet she's plenty important," he said, chuckling. "Trevor, here, is just too much the gentleman to kiss and tell, aren't you, Hughes?"

I stood and began packing my recorder, shoving the tapes in after it with quick angry jabs. "You know, Solly, I put up with you in school because you were always good for a few laughs. Well, you're not funny anymore. You're just a pompous windbag with a lot of money to throw around. I've got news for you, *pal*, it doesn't impress me."

Solly jumped to his feet, face mottled pink. "Just one fucking minute, Hughes! I worked hard for that dough. And I couldn't give a rat's ass what you think. You owe us!"

"For what? Just because I know something you don't, you feel you have the *right* to know it?"

"No! Because Harlan was the best friend I ever had, and I want to know why he fucking died! Is that so fucking hard for Mr. Big-Shot Writer to understand?"

"Guys, please!" Ken said, his hang-dog face crimped with worry. "This isn't the place."

Solly turned on Ken, his mouth twisted into a snarl. "The hell it isn't."

"He's right, Ken."

They both turned to me, expressions registering mild surprise. It was a picture that under any other circumstances would have made me laugh. Now, I was just too damned tired. "You *do* have a right to know, as much as any of us. But you don't have the right to unreasonably demand it. We've all had a bit too much to drink, and it's late. How about we meet here tomorrow morning?"

"For a little hair of the dog?" Ken asked.

I did smile then.

"Sure, Ken. You bring the dog."

Solly grinned and clapped me on the shoulder. "Sorry about the 'kiss and tell' crack, I didn't mean it."

"Yes, you did, Solly. The thing is, you're right about that, too. I *am* too much of a gentleman."

Without another word, I picked up my briefcase and left them. Outside, the air had turned cool and I hurried to the taxi stand near the corner. One of these days I was going to have to break down and buy a car, but not having one was one of those quirks of mine. Besides, in Boston, I didn't really need one.

The ride back to Charlestown was blessedly quick and uneventful. I paid the driver and gave him a generous tip, at least he thought it was, streaking away with a wave and a wide grin plastered on his ebony face.

The inside of my condo felt cold and damp, like an ancient tomb. It was an apt comparison. Until I'd met Madeleine I was entombed, and now I felt more isolated than ever. I fought the urge to go down to that friendly little blue-collar dive around the corner, realizing that giving into it was the first step down a long and torturous road—a road dotted with lonely drunken nights punctuated by ceaseless bouts of self-pity. The thought of that, and of Captain Pierce's poignant story, took away all desire for alcohol.

Shivering from more than just the cold, I turned up the heat, shambled over to the couch, and dropped into it, suddenly aware I wasn't a bit sleepy and that the night's endless hours stretched before me. I glanced at my computer, remembering that I'd been incommunicado for a number of days.

"Any messages, Milly?"

"*Representatives from the five major networks called—three times. Your agent, Marty, also has called twice, as well as an attorney for the estate of Harlan Astor.*"

I sat up when I heard that last one. "Play Marty's last message first."

"*Engaging surround sound,*" Milly said.

The monitor snapped on a moment later, revealing Marty looking uncharacteristically agitated.

"Trevor, are you there?" Marty appeared to be searching the screen for me. "Trevor, if you're there, I want you to call me back right away. Mannheim Books is going nuts! Nuts, you hear me? They want the book pronto, said they would bump their current print schedule for you. Trevor? Goddamn it, you call me back! They want the book on the shelves in three fucking weeks! I got them to triple the advance, and I've already got these suits from La-La land sniffing around the movie rights. You hit the jackpot, kid. Call me."

Marty rang off and the screen turned black. I should have been ecstatic, delirious—but I felt only a great empty hole in my gut, as if everything had been scooped out. The original advance Marty negotiated was a solid six figures. If what he'd said was true, and I had no reason to doubt him, it would now be over 1.5 million. A little more than one quarter of one percent of what my late friend had spent on his Quixotic vision. Normally, I would have been doing cartwheels. Now, I couldn't care less. And writing the book was about the last thing I wanted to do.

"Do you wish to hear the other messages?" Milly said with infinite patience.

I shoved Marty from my mind; I would deal with him later.

"Play back the lawyer's message, Milly."

"Executing."

The black screen was replaced by the image of an attractive middle-aged woman wearing a navy power suit, paisley tie, horn-rimmed glasses, and a sober expression. "This is a message for..." she bent her head down, as if consulting notes. "...Mr. Trevor Hughes. Mr. Hughes, my name is Jane Hurdigger, and it is quite imperative that you call me immediately. I can be reached at 212-555-5150. If I'm not there, my computer will page me. Good day."

"Shall I dial the number, Trevor?"

"Sure, and while you're at it, why don't you talk to her."

Milly was silent. I don't know if it was confusion on her part or disapproval. Either way, it was up to me. "Dial it, Milly," I said. "But turn off my camera."

"Executing."

The eleven digits rattled off in a flurry of musical tones and a moment later, I heard it ring. At the fifth ring, I was about to tell Milly to hang up when the screen faded up on the woman seated on an expensive sofa, the area next to her piled with legal pads and law books. It looked as if she took her work home, as well.

Behind her, I could see the New York skyline. She had to be on the fiftieth floor, at least, judging from the view. And from what little I could see of her apartment: an expensive mixture of Laura Ashley and Chippendale, the woman knew her way around the legal profession. Of course, she would have to if she'd been retained by Harlan.

She frowned at the screen. "Hello, is anyone there?"

"Ms. Hurdigger, this is Trevor Hughes."

"Is something wrong with your camera, Mr. Hughes?"

"No, I'm just out of the shower."

I saw her flush at my lie, and that brought a smile to my lips. "What can I do for you, Ms. Hurdigger?"

She became all business then. "Yes, I wanted to get in touch with you about Mr. Astor's will."

"What about it?"

"You're in it, Mr. Hughes."

This surprised the hell out of me, and I was still churning that around in my brain when the attorney spoke again.

"Mr. Hughes, it really would be easier if we could see each other."

"Milly, turn on the camera."

The monitor snapped on and her expression relaxed. "Ahh, that's better. Now, let me see...."

If she'd noticed that I was fully dressed, she kept her reaction to herself.

"...Yes, here it is. Mr. Astor placed a new codicil to his will prior to his untimely demise. Simply put, Mr. Hughes, Mr. Astor has bequeathed you several of his New York properties, worth by our recent appraisals at about $400 million dollars."

My expression must have baffled her, as did my silence, for she removed her glasses and frowned with concern. "Are you all right, Mr. Hughes?"

"What are the properties?"

"A block of town houses in Gramercy Park, I—"

"Sell them."

The attorney looked startled. "I'm sorry, Mr. Hughes, did you say—"

"Sell them, yes."

"Mr. Hughes, those properties are in one of the most exclusive areas in Manhattan."

"I know exactly where they are. Is there a problem with my selling them?"

"No, there shouldn't be. But they are income property. Mr. Astor realized at least $20 million a year from them. Are you sure you still wish to sell them?"

"Yes."

"Very well, I will contact Mr. Astor's agent, though the sale may take a little time. The market is sluggish these days."

"I'm not in a hurry. You'll stay in touch?"

"Of course, Mr. Hughes."

"Good-bye, then."

She started to say something else, and I cut her off with the push of a button on the manual remote. I shook my head, squeezing my eyes shut. It seemed that everyone wanted to give me money today. Too bad it wouldn't cure what ailed me.

Leaning back on the sofa, my eyes fell upon my briefcase containing the DVD recorder and the disks. Without thinking, I reached for it, pulling out the recorder.

There was only one disk I wanted to review. I held Madeleine's DVD in my hand. It weighed barely an ounce and was the only tangible part of her that remained. I didn't even have a picture of her. My vision blurred with tears and a part of me wanted to fling it against the wall— do anything to end the pain I felt. Instead, I opened the jewel box, pulled out the disk and placed it in the recorder.

A moment later, it began....

TUESDAY
APRIL 10, 2012

7

I left the wheelhouse a few minutes after Captain Pierce and walked the few steps to the radio room. Aside from the luxuries that Harlan's money had purchased, he'd spared no expense in recreating bygone technology. The radio room, or rather, the Marconi Room, was in every sense a museum piece. Not only were the metal and wood components of the Marconi Wireless reconstructed to perfection, but he'd gone out of his way to re-manufacture certain vacuum tubes that no longer existed, tubes unique to the Marconi system.

I found the wireless operator sitting at the radio, monitoring the radio traffic, the heavy Bakelite headphones clamped to his head. He saw me and smiled, lifting them off.

"Yes, sir, can I help you?"

The man's thick British accent sounded as if he'd originally come from somewhere up north, I guessed Manchester, or thereabouts.

"Can you really send anything on that?" I asked, pointing to the Marconi.

"Right you are. The range is nowhere near what a digital model can do, but it works."

Since the Marconi company no longer existed, I had arranged with a friend, who dabbled in ham radio, and knew Morse code, to receive my dispatches. He also managed a website, and would be responsible for formatting them to look like hundred-year-old wireless messages and placing them into our own website. It was Marty's idea to call it:

www.titanic-2012.com. I just hoped the novelty wouldn't wear off too fast.

"Do you wish to send a message, sir?" the Marconi operator asked.

"Uhh, yes," I said, pulling out notes I'd made prior to boarding. I looked them over. "Would it be better if I wrote it down, or dictated it?"

"Either way is fine, but I can key faster if I'm hearing it."

I nodded.

"Okay, then, let's give it a try."

"The name's Richards, by the way, Sammy Richards," he said, indicating the chair next to him.

I shook his hand and sat down. "Well, Sammy, this is likely to take a little while."

"All right by me. Seems I'm not as popular as I'd hoped."

He gave a sheepish shrug and turned to the wireless, adjusting the frequency with a slight twist of a large black knob. I felt sorry for him. On the voyage of the original *Titanic*, wireless communications were in their infancy, a novelty the passengers exploited to the fullest, sending frivolous messages to loved ones. A century later, in the Digital Age, it was little more than a curiosity, a museum piece. And yet, if anything were to go wrong, it might be our only lifeline.

I nodded to him that I was ready and began: "They say history repeats itself and that all things that go around, come around. Well, today that is certainly the case. I am writing to you from the Marconi room just behind the bridge on the *R.M.S. Titanic....*"

Twenty minutes later we were done, a total of a thousand words, far more than a real Marconigram. And I'd done a fair job of dictating, something I'd never liked doing. Milly, my computer, was easily capable of taking dictation as fast as I could speak, and of telling the difference between words like "there" and "their." But I liked to have my hands on the keys. Besides the fact that I thought better doing it manually, it also felt more like writing. I suppose I'm old fashioned in some ways. Perhaps that was why Harlan's dream had seduced me.

Tucking my notes away, I thanked Sammy and left the Marconi Room. My next stop was Harlan's stateroom. I'd wanted to have him take me on a tour of the ship, and to interview him. No matter who else I might talk to about their reasons for coming on the *Titanic*, the book would not be complete without an interview with the man behind it all.

But it was not to be, at least not then.

I read something once, I forget where, that fate will always step in when you least expect it, and this was just such a time. When I left the Marconi Room, something made me turn toward the bow. Maybe it was the way the sun, now much lower in the water and turning a fiery orange, was glinting off the water. Or maybe it was simply that I wanted another look at the *Titanic's* magnificent prow as it sliced the waves, heading toward Cherbourg. Whatever it was ceased to matter as soon as I saw her.

From two-hundred feet away, she looked childlike, fragile. She stood at the tip of the bow, feet firmly planted in the railings, arms outstretched at her sides. The wind billowed her dress and the shawl intertwined in her arms, making her appear as if she were about to take wing. I smiled then, both entranced and not a little amused.

The woman was imitating the famous "flying" scene from the movie; the only thing missing was a Leonardo DiCaprio stand-in embracing her from behind. The odd thing was that it seemed perfectly natural, and the only thing that *did* surprise me was that there wasn't a line of women behind her waiting their turn.

With my previous intentions forgotten for the moment, I took the stairs down to C-Deck, which lay on the same level as the Well Deck, the area just aft of the forecastle. I passed between the two electric cranes and took one of the two sets of stairs leading up to the forecastle.

At the top of the stairs, I threaded my way past the Number One hatch, the steam winches and the capstans, my eyes fixed on the woman. The wind seemed stronger when I neared the bow, and I bent into it, careful to avoid tripping over the auxiliary anchor, a solid piece of cast iron weighing in at fifteen tons resting in a recessed niche just aft of the bow peak.

The closer I drew to her, the more self-conscious I became, not knowing what I would say, if anything. She still hadn't moved from her position: arms out from her body, her head thrown back, eyes closed, her expression serene. She had a classic beauty, a profile like that of an old cameo broach: A sharp, well-shaped nose sat above full lips curved in an enigmatic smile. And though her eyes were closed, I imagined them to be a deep emerald green contrasting perfectly with her thick mane of auburn hair. The wind whipped it about her face, but she seemed oblivious, almost in a trance.

I was about to go, not wanting to disturb her, when she spoke.

"Don't say it," she said.

Her voice startled me, a sweet contralto, like music carried on a summer breeze.

"Excuse me?"

"I know what you're thinking. Don't say it."

Her smile widened and she opened her eyes and turned to me. My breath caught in my throat. They *were* green, so green they almost glowed.

"You *were* thinking that, weren't you?"

"I—I don't know what I was thinking." I blurted, feeling like a tongue-tied schoolboy.

"Oh, surely you've got *something* going on in that handsome head of yours?"

She turned and started to climb down, and I moved to help her, grasping her hands in mine. Her skin felt cool, and slightly dry, no doubt from the prolonged exposure to the wind and sun. She wobbled a moment before steadying herself.

"Careful," I said, "it's a long way down."

"Thank you, my Galahad," she said, leaping to the deck.

Now that we were on the same level, I saw that she was about six inches shorter than me, forcing her to look up to make eye contact. At this proximity those emerald eyes caught me in their vibrant splendor.

"To tell you the truth, I was wondering why you were the only one doing that."

She laughed, a great burst of sound that brought a smile to my lips in spite of my nervousness.

"Oh, God, I just had this image of a long line and someone selling tickets, hah!"

I laughed, too, the image even sillier than the one I'd conjured. "Well, you really made a beautiful picture up there. You looked just like her—like Kate Winslet."

She studied me a moment, as if trying to determine whether I was really serious, or simply being flirtatious. Then she grinned.

"Wasn't she lovely at the christening?"

"You were there?" I said, surprised.

She nodded. "I felt like her, just now. For a brief moment I felt as light as the air, as if I could actually take off and soar...." She spun in place, her dress billowing out, laughing again. "It was so wonderfully...transcendent. Do you believe in transcendence?"

My expression must have been comical, for she laughed again. "I guess you're one of those cynical old stick-in-the-muds, hmmm?"

"I don't know about being a stick-in-the-mud, but cynical is just about right."

"That's too bad, cynics miss out on so much."

"I disagree, I don't think we've missed anything. That's the problem, we've seen too much. Besides, don't you know that all cynics are failed romantics?"

"Is that what you are? A failed romantic? No one waiting at home?"

"No, I'm afraid not," I said, a wave of sadness stealing over me. "She and I—We didn't see things the same way."

She covered her mouth in embarrassment. "Oh, God, I'm sorry, I didn't mean to stir anything up for you."

"You didn't. I'm fine; I'm dealing with it."

"That may be, but I shouldn't be so blunt. It seems I'm always just saying whatever comes into my silly head. And here I am asking these personal questions, and I don't even know your name." She giggled.

I smiled.

"Believe me, I'm enjoying every moment. It's refreshing. I'm Trevor Hughes, by the way."

"Madeleine Regehr, but please...call me, Maddy."

She stuck out her hand, and I took it, surprised by the firmness of her grip. With most women shaking hands felt as if one were grasping a limp rag. It was that firm grip and the frank intelligence behind her eyes that caused me to be more forward than I normally would have been.

"I know this is going to sound a little strange, but would you mind if I interviewed you? I'm writing a book."

Her eyes widened. "Now, I know who you are! You seemed so familiar, and your name, too. I just couldn't put it together until now. You're the mystery writer Mr. Astor told us about. I'm really honored to meet you."

I felt my face flush. "Now, you're embarrassing me."

Her expression became sly. "Something I'm very good at, I'm afraid."

"About the interview...."

She shook her head, emphatic. "I'm sorry, but I don't want to be a part of your experiment."

"I really wouldn't call it that. I just want to know why you wanted to come on this voyage. It's something I'm asking everyone."

"I would think the answer was obvious," she said, nodding toward her perch on the bow.

"Sure, but I think, for most people, it goes a lot deeper than the film. At least it has for the Captain."

"So, you've already talked to him?" she asked, curiosity evident in the gentle arch of her brow.

"And it was fairly painless."

"For him, or for you?"

I held up my hands.

"If you don't want to talk to me, that's fine. I have no problem with that."

"I absolutely do want to talk to you. I just would rather we do it as friends...not as something so...remote."

"All right, " I said, suddenly shivering from the chill wind that had sprung up. "But how about we go inside. It's getting cold and I'd like to take a walk through the ship. I've been so busy, I haven't had a moment, until now."

That sly look was back on her face. "I've been through it twice already. How about I give you the ten-cent tour?"

"Deal."

Grabbing me by the hand, she led me up the stairs up to the boat deck, where we took a quick peek into the gymnasium. The quaint-looking rowing machines and stationary bikes were a far cry from the modern machines I was used to seeing. They looked dangerous. From there we descended to the poop deck, the aftermost part of the ship, passing several large groups of other passengers who looked to be equally enthralled with exploring the vessel.

At the stern, we spent a few minutes staring over the railing at the wake created by the ship's triple screws, and then made our way forward. She must have read my mind, for we headed next to the First Class Dining Saloon. Stewards puttered about, busily setting the tables for the evening meal with fresh starched linen, hand-painted china and the sterling flatware stamped with the White Star emblem. From there, we made our way through the reception room to the Grand Staircase. I ran my hand down the polished oak handrail, marveling at its silky gloss, the wrought-iron balustrade with its gold accents taking my breath away. In my mind's eye, I could see young Kate Winslet descending, resplendent in her gown, her eyes locked with Leonardo DiCaprio's waiting at the bottom like a young Adonis.

Maddy and I took the stairs down to E-deck and then down into the bowels of the ship, stopping to explore the hold. Holding hands, we threaded our way through tons of crates piled to the ceiling.

"It's all fake, you know," Maddy said. "Engine rooms are this way." She nodded toward a door at the far end.

"Why?"

"Don't you want to see the engines?"

"No, no," I said, shaking my head. "Why is the cargo fake?"

Maddy gave me a strange look, then shrugged. "I guess your friend didn't want an empty room. Come on, slowpoke, let's go."

She took off ahead, and I had to speed up to a trot to keep up. She chattered on about the marvels of the ship's engines, but my mind still turned on her comment about the cargo. It bothered me. And while I could appreciate Harlan's single-minded desire for authenticity, I found this last detail stretched what bounds were left of credibility. Fake cargo? It didn't fit. So, I made a mental note to ask Harlan about it later.

The reciprocating engine room, one of the largest open areas on the ship, was marvel of cyclopean engineering. Monstrous pistons shot up and down, turning on cam shafts the diameter of sewer pipes. Crewmen known as "greasers" and "oilers", tended the colossal machinery, making sure everything remained well-lubricated and ran smoothly, all under the watchful eyes of the Engine Room Officers standing stiffly by the brass commutators.

As for the boiler rooms, they took me completely by surprise. Instead of the anterooms to Hell I'd expected, they were almost antiseptic. And eerily deserted. No sweat-drenched men shoveling coal into fiery maws, only silent pipes leading directly into the burners.

"Isn't it marvelous?" Maddy shouted. "It's all oil-fueled."

It *was* marvelous. It was also perplexing. Harlan had been so adamant about authenticity. Why had he opted for oil-fueled boilers, rather than ones that burned coal? Unless it was because of pollution regulations. With scientists increasingly up in arms about global warming, and governments stiffening their laws, it was not an unreasonable choice. Burning coal was a lot dirtier than oil. Besides, I realized, who would want to spend the voyage of their dreams shoveling coal? Maddy tugged at my sleeve.

"Let's go forward," she said, pointing toward the bow. I nodded. As amazing as the engine and boiler rooms were, I was all for leaving its sweltering and cacophonous environs behind.

Moving up a deck, we passed through the third class dining room, so bare and utilitarian compared to the Jacobean elegance of the First Class Saloon. Next came the Turkish bath and the swimming pool, its chlorinated coolness inviting. Then it was down two decks to the mail room and the forward holds.

More of the fake cargo greeted us, though one of the pieces made me laugh. It was a 1912 Renault, much like the one from the film, in which Rose, the heroine, loses her virginity to Jack Dawson. Maddy saw the amusement in my eyes.

"I guess there ought to be a ticket booth for this one, too?"

"That's the funny thing, Maddy. I've been watching everyone from the time we all boarded, and while we were walking through the ship. Nobody's with anybody. There are no couples, and I find that odd. As odd as finding a beautiful woman like you alone on this ship."

Maddy didn't say anything, her expression unreadable.

"I'm sorry, I guess it's my turn to put my foot in it. Did I hit a nerve?"

She turned to me, smiling wistfully. "Maybe...once.... But not now." She put her arm through mine. "Now, my Galahad, would you please escort me to the bow?"

I could tell that something bothered her. Maybe she and a boyfriend had booked passage together, and they'd broken up days or weeks before the sailing. It was a plausible scenario, considering what had happened between Julia and me. I decided to let it go, but it made me want to know her all the more. Perhaps, if she got to know me better, she would change her mind about that interview. There also was a part of me that wanted to assuage her wounds—to take away whatever pain lived within her. And that very thought scared me to the core, because I'd never felt that way with Julia.

We'd just passed Boiler Room Six and entered the first-class baggage holds, when I spied a lone crewman standing guard at one of the watertight doors up ahead. He stood well over six feet in height, had a bulky mesomorphic frame practically bursting out of his uniform, and looked as if he'd pumped himself up further with steroids.

He stiffened when we approached. "I'm sorry, Sir, Miss, but this area's off-limits to passengers."

He glared at me, and I felt a curious emotion: a mixture of anger and embarrassment. It was the kind of lethal mixture that, with an attractive woman present, might ignite tempers. I kept my cool.

Aside from towering over me, the man had to outweigh me by at least fifty pounds. If I tangled with him, I'd likely end up as hamburger.

And for what? What was behind door number one? Hell, it was probably more empty crates, and hardly worth the risk of bodily harm.

Then again, if that were the case, if it *was* only empty boxes, why post a man to guard it? No, it was probably something personal to

Harlan, something of great value, and that meant it was none of my business.

"Come on, let's go," I said.

But Maddy would have none of it. She walked up to the man, staring him down with a glare of her own. "You know, it's one thing to keep us out of there, but it's quite another to be so rude. Life's too short."

The man blanched at those last words and I saw him deflate, his expression turning grave. "I—I'm sorry, Miss, it's orders, you see. I didn't mean nothing by it."

I saw a look of understanding pass between them, and then Maddy came back to me. We started to leave and then she stopped and turned. "What's your name, sailor?"

The man looked worried for a moment, then spoke. "Charlie, Charlie Nelson.

"Well, Charlie, Charlie Nelson, try not to work too hard, okay?"

A smile flitted across the big man's face. "You, too, Miss."

We returned to E-deck and took one of the lifts up three levels to B-deck. It was now a quarter past six, and we were due to dock at Cherbourg at any moment. We would lay in the harbor for approximately two hours, weighing anchor at ten past eight for the journey to the Irish port of Cobh, known as Queenstown in 1912. After a brief stay there, it would be due west into the vast Atlantic. The new *Titanic* was retracing its ancestor's original route, though it would take on no new passengers.

Outside the lift, I turned to Maddy.

"I want to thank you for the tour. It was infinitely more enjoyable than it would have been alone."

She smiled, revealing white, even teeth. "You're welcome, Galahad. Thanks for rescuing me."

"From what?"

"Boredom.... You've been fun."

"Me?" I said, exaggerating my reaction.

"Yes, you, Mr. Cynical," she said, chucking me on the shoulder. The playful punch turned into an affectionate squeeze on my forearm.

I could tell from the look in her eyes that she didn't want the afternoon's idyll to end. Neither did I. She'd cast a spell on me without conscious effort, just by being herself.

"Can I walk you to your stateroom?" I asked.

"Not unless you want to go back to E-deck."

"E-deck?"

Maddy laughed. "You look so surprised."

"I guess I am. I just didn't figure you for a steerage girl. You seemed so—"

"Snooty, stuck-up, full of myself?" Her grin widened, belying her mock anger.

"Well, maybe a little...."

"Now, wait a minute!"

We both laughed then. "Seriously, I just assumed. I guess that makes me the ass," I said.

"Not at all. It's only for tonight, anyway. I'm moving up to second class tomorrow. I thought it would be interesting to work my way up to first class."

"This ship is so empty it shouldn't be a problem. I don't know why Harlan didn't fill it. He actually told me that he'd turned people away. Doesn't that seem strange to you?"

Maddy shrugged, suddenly distracted. "It's his ship. He can do whatever he wants, I suppose. I'm just glad he let me come." Her eyes moistened and she blinked rapidly.

"Are you okay?" I asked, alarmed.

"I'm fine, Trevor. I guess I'm just a little tired. I'll see you at dinner, okay?"

"Of course," I replied, taking her hand and kissing it. "I saw this in a movie once, and I always wanted to do it."

When she didn't laugh, I stood up and let go of her hand, watching while she retraced her steps back to the lift. The operator shut the gate, and a moment later she dropped from sight. It was then I realized that she'd called me Trevor for the first time. And the feeling that gave me was like an electrical charge racing through my body. Fate had indeed stepped in when I wasn't looking, and I was in big trouble....

8

One of the other three lifts appeared a moment later, disgorging two elderly women, one holding a Pekingese in her arms. The tiny dog had a pink ribbon tied between its twitching ears, and it eyed me with wide-eyed terror, as if I were some unknown predator bent on devouring it.

Smiling at the two women, I entered the lift and the operator ran me up to B-deck with uncommon swiftness. I was just drawing my door key when I spied a steward standing outside the door to Harlan's suite, and I suddenly remembered my original intention to speak with him. I slipped the heavy skeleton key back into my pocket and walked down the hall.

"Excuse me, sir," the steward said, raising a hand toward me, "Mr. Astor has requested that he not be disturbed."

The steward had a chubby face full of freckles and a thick London accent.

"Could you please tell him that Trevor Hughes needs to speak with him?"

The steward eyed me with an expression that made me feel as if I were an impertinent child. "I'm sorry, sir, he was *quite* explicit."

I frowned, concerned. It wasn't like Harlan to hole up in his stateroom like a hermit, especially after all the money he'd spent to recreate this magnificent ship. The man I knew would be out among his guests reveling in the spotlight.

I opened my mouth to offer a snappy comeback, then thought better of it. The steward was only doing his job, and would no doubt become belligerent should I persist. I smiled and shrugged my shoulders with practiced indifference. "Okay, could you tell him I stopped by?"

The steward nodded, a patronizing smile sliding onto his face. "Certainly, sir. It would be my pleasure."

Back inside my stateroom, I found that the set of tails had been removed from the closet and laid out on the bed, as were my underwear, socks, and a pair of patent leather slippers, so shiny they looked wet. In addition, the pearl cufflinks and collar studs were inserted into the correct holes. Obviously, my steward had preceded me into the room. A part of me felt privileged, as would any Edwardian traveling first class. The twenty-first century man in me felt invaded.

A knock sounded at the door and I opened it. A steward stood outside, his white jacket immaculate. "Yes?"

"Good evening, Mr. Hughes, I'm your Steward, Henry Llewellyn." He bent at the waist, giving me a vestigial bow and strode into the room, forcing me to move aside. "I've come to draw your bath."

"My bath?" I asked, too dazed to realize that I'd shut the door out of sheer habit.

"But of course, sir," he said, looking arch. "You *do* want to freshen up before dinner?"

The man oozed unctuous charm, reminding me of the character from an old 1980s television show, *Mr. Belvedere*. And, in a way, the man had the same look about him: tall and beefy, with gray hair topping a jowly face practiced in looking besieged.

"Mr. Llewellyn—"

"Please, sir, call me Henry."

"Sorry. Henry, I was not aware that stewards aboard the *Titanic* functioned as personal valets."

An indulgent smile played across his lips.

"No, sir, normally they do not. However—"

I raised my hand. "Don't tell me...Mr. Astor hired you to attend to my needs. Is that about right?"

Henry bowed again. "Quite."

"And I suppose you were the one who laid out my evening clothes?"

"Right again, sir."

"All right," I said, throwing up my hands. "I guess I'm just going to have to grin and bear it."

"Very good, sir." Henry turned toward the bathroom.

"Uhh, Henry?"

"Yes, sir?"

"Just one thing. And don't take this the wrong way, because it has more to do with me than you. I would appreciate it in the future if you would not enter my stateroom when I am not present."

"But, Mr. Hughes, if I am to do my job—"

I raised my hand again, and his mouth clamped shut. I couldn't tell if he was angry or bewildered. Maybe it was a little bit of both.

"Shall I draw the bath, sir?"

"By all means, Henry."

He disappeared into the bathroom and a moment later I heard the rush of water filling the tub. When he didn't come out right away, I had the sickening feeling that I was expected to bathe with him in the room, or worse, that he expected to bathe me himself. I was relieved to see him emerge a second later.

"When you are ready to dress, sir, please ring the buzzer next to your bed."

Here was where I drew the line.

"That's okay, Henry, I won't be needing you for that. I'm much too old and far too American to be dressed by anyone but me."

I thought I saw a tiny smile flicker across his craggy face. "Very well, sir. If you need anything...." He left the rest unsaid and exited the room, shutting the door behind him with a soft click.

Shaking my head in amazement at Harlan's continuing largesse, I threw off my clothes, tossing them onto one of the Biedermeier chairs and padded into the bathroom. Unlike the rest of the stateroom, the bathroom was a study in elegant simplicity: bare white walls, marble washbasin with gold-plated fixtures, hexagonal tile floors, and pipes running along the walls and ceiling. The tub, a cavernous affair stood on clawed feet against the wall opposite the toilet, steam rising from it in a thick cloud. I sniffed it, detecting the pungent aroma of bath oil.

I was beginning to wonder if Harlan wasn't perpetrating another of his infamous gags. First the Polish prostitute, now a valet. I could only guess at what might be next.

I slid into the water, feeling the heat tingle my skin and hissing with pleasure. Settling back, I took a soaked washcloth and draped it over my eyes, suddenly glad for the silence and feel of the water lapping at my chin. After twenty minutes, I sprayed myself with cold water and toweled off.

The set of 1912 tails proved to be trickier than I'd imagined. The collar, so starched that the fabric felt like plastic, refused to stay on the front stud. Just when I thought I had it pegged, and would grab for the tie, it sprang loose, flapping outward like something from an old silent movie. I finally managed to make it stay long enough to get the tie around my neck. Then it took me the better part of fifteen minutes of frustration before I realized that I had no hope of tying the bow correctly. Feeling foolish, I walked over and pressed the little black button set into the dark paneling between the door and the bed.

I only had to wait about two minutes before the knock came. "Come in, Henry," I said.

The steward bustled in, assessing the situation in a single glance. With swift practiced moves, he had the tie knotted in less than thirty seconds. And what's more, he'd done it facing me, which meant that he'd tied it "backwards."

"You're a handy man to have around, Henry," I said, not a little impressed.

"So, they tell me, sir," he replied, helping me on with my vest.

Unlike modern evening clothes, which stressed function over form and tended more to the "false front," this vest was a full vest with a piqued front, satin back, and real mother of pearl buttons. The jacket, with its peaked satin-faced lapels, fitted perfectly, and even though the lapels were far narrower than were the current fashion, they looked sharp, as did the functioning buttons on the sleeves. I examined myself in the full-length mirror attached to the back of the bathroom door, secretly glad I'd stayed trim. Edwardian styles were extremely unforgiving to the portly frame.

Slipping into the shoes, I turned to Henry, who gave an approving nod. "Quite the fashion plate, sir."

"Thank you, Henry. Now, if I can keep from spilling the soup on it, I will consider it a successful evening."

"I should think that would be easy for you, sir," he said, with a tiny grin. "Shall I turn down your bed?"

I nodded, making ready to leave the room. A quick glance at the clock revealed that it was now half past seven. Time for a quick stop at the First Class Lounge.

Whoever had designed the original *Titanic* had not spared anything when it came to the public rooms for first-class passengers. This was especially true of the lounge. Decorated in a modified Louis Quinze Versailles style that dazzled the eyes with its rococo details, it boasted enough floor space to accommodate nearly the entire first class population.

When I entered it around 7:35, it held a smattering of perhaps fifty individuals assembled in groups of various sizes. I scanned the men trying to see if Harlan was among them. I didn't find him, so I grabbed a whiskey at the bar, savoring its dark peaty flavor while watching a group of men playing poker.

Some of the women also watched, and I was impressed at their attention to their period costume: beaded gowns predominated, as did ones sporting volumes of lace. And judging from their stiff, regal bearing, they'd also elected to wear authentic corsets, which must have been excruciating. For the first time since parting from her at the elevators, I thought of Maddy, trying to conjure a mental picture of how she would look.

At 7:55, I retraced my steps to the Grand Staircase and followed the crowd down to D-deck and the Dining Saloon.

Once touted as the largest dining room afloat, the Saloon was nearly as wide as the entire ship and stretched a hundred feet in length, resplendent in its *faux* Jacobean paneling and detailed plaster work.

Every table glowed with the bright chatter of its inhabitants, as well as the dazzling array of silver flatware, lead crystal and hand-painted china.

I found Harlan seated at a table for six, holding court as he always did, his rapt audience spellbound by an inexhaustible supply of anecdotes. Every chair was filled save for two directly to his right. I was threading my way through the sea of tables when he looked up and smiled, spotting me.

"Trev!" he said, grinning. "You look great! You could—"

I held up a hand. "Almost pass for a gentleman, I know."

We laughed and embraced. "You've got to stop doing this, Harlan. A valet, for Christ's sake? You're going to spoil me."

He held me at arm's length.

"Jesus, if I don't spoil you, who will?"

He laughed again, and the rest of the table joined him. I felt my face redden. Good-natured or not, I was never comfortable being the butt of a joke.

Harlan slapped me on the back. "Everybody, this is my friend, Trevor Hughes."

One by one, he introduced me to my fellow diners. There was Hoyt Asbury, a stout mustachioed retiree from Brighton, who sat sipping a vodka tonic with a sour look on his face. He barely acknowledged me.

Next to him was, Gavin Reynolds, an ascetic young man, whose pale translucent skin and white-blonde hair made him look like an albino. He wasn't, of course, as his deep liquid brown eyes attested. He gave me a friendly nod and raised his glass of white wine.

Lastly, there was Hermione Bates, a lively widow from Kent, who appeared ill at ease trussed up in her corseted gown. She smiled when she heard my name, her narrow face lighting up. "I absolutely love your mysteries, Mr. Hughes. When are we going to see another? I do so love that Conrad Holm. So devil-may-care."

"I've just finished the manuscript for the latest one. But it won't be out for about six months, I'm afraid."

"Oh, dear, what a shame. I would have loved reading it. Mr. Astor tells me that you're writing one about this voyage. And that you're interviewing the passengers?"

"That's right."

"How nice," she said, her eyes flicking to Harlan, then back to me. "I hope you'll be kind."

I found that an odd thing to say, but let it pass.

"Perhaps you'd allow me interview you later?" I said.

The woman shook her head. "Oh, I'd be such a bore, really."

"Nonsense. I'm sure you'd have a lot to tell."

"Now, now, Trev," Harlan said. "Let's not bother Mrs. Bates with any more business. I say we enjoy the evening."

"Yes, let's," Asbury said, stifling a belch.

Picking up my napkin, I noticed the still-empty chair to my right. I turned to Harlan, indicating it with a nod of my head. "Are we still expecting someone?"

"Well, you never know who might turn up," he said, giving me a conspiratorial wink.

My rejoinder died on my lips when Maddy swept through the double doors at the far end of the room. She wore a tight-fitting short-sleeved floor-length gown of bottle-green silk, set off with abalone beading. The neckline, a deep scoop with an iridescent gold fringe, stayed well above her decolletage. And she'd piled her luxurious auburn hair atop her head in a Psyche knot, reminding me of the Gibson Girl. With her glowing milk-white skin, the entire effect was one of elegance blended with eroticism.

An eon seemed to pass while all of this tumbled through my mind, and then I snapped back to reality when I saw her eyes searching the room, an air of expectancy about her. A part of me silently prayed that I had something to do with that.

"Excuse me a minute, Harlan," I said, standing up. Conscious only of Maddy, I crossed the room, dodging white-jacketed stewards bearing heavy silver trays piled high with epicurean delights. When I was twenty feet away from her, she turned to me and smiled. My feet felt as if I'd walked off the edge of a cliff and the din of dishes and human chatter faded, replaced by the pounding of my pulse.

"Oh, Trevor, you look so nice, so debonair," she said.

Coming from anyone else that line would have sounded commonplace and trite. From her, it sounded as heartfelt and sincere as I knew it to be. I found my voice, though to me it sounded hoarse and rough as sandpaper. "My God, Maddy, you—you look...absolutely stunning...."

Her smile brightened and she moved closer to me, her eyes shining. "You really are a Galahad. You always know just what to say."

"And for you I mean every word."

She nodded. "I know...."

I held out my arm. "Shall we repair to our table and dazzle them with our presence, my dear?" I asked, putting on a fake English accent.

Maddy laughed, and we started back to the table. All during that short walk, I was conscious of more than a few male eyes following our progress. On the one hand, I was flattered to be seen in the company of such a beautiful woman. And the fact that it was Maddy, made it all the finer. On the other hand, I had to admit to a sense of quiet panic, that someone else might vie for her affections.

While I held out her chair and watched her seat herself with such unaffected grace, it all hit with the force of a hammer blow: *I wanted her to want me.* In the worst way.

Suddenly frightened at the intensity of these feelings welling up inside me, I took my chair, momentarily subdued. Maddy noticed.

"Are you okay?"

"I'm fine," I lied. "Just a little too much sun today."

The steward assigned to our table introduced himself and handed out the menus, and I made a great pretense of studying mine while attempting to sort out my muddled thoughts.

I saw Harlan gloating out of the corner of my eye, and turned to him. "You arranged this, too, didn't you?" I asked him, grinning slyly.

His eyes widened in mock surprise. "Me? Now, wherever did you get such an idea, kiddo?" He laughed then, and I made out another mental IOU to add to the mounting pile. One good thing. Even if Harlan meant to spoil me, Maddy would help me to keep it all in perspective.

The waiter began taking orders and I returned my attention to the menu. In honor of the original *Titanic*, Harlan had arranged to have our first night's meal use the same menu as was served on that last fateful night in 1912. It was a full eleven courses, and while I knew that I would never be able to eat it all, I intended to savor a bit from each dish, so I ordered with a cavalier abandon, starting with the Canapés á l'Amiral, through the Consommé, four rich entrees with a sorbet in between each one, a salad, a cold paté dish, finally ending with Peaches in Chartreuse Jelly, a sort of proto-Jell-O for the Edwardian set.

When the steward left with the orders, the Sommelier stepped forward. "Would you like to choose the wines, *Monsieur* Astor?" he asked.

Harlan clapped me on the shoulder and announced to the others: "I'll have you good people know, that aside from being a crackerjack writer, Trevor's quite the wine connoisseur. Aren't you, kiddo?"

I shrugged, trying not to let the embarrassment I felt show on my face. Under the table, I felt Maddy squeeze my hand. Somehow that made it both better and worse at the same time.

"Are you really?" Mrs. Bates asked, trying to adjust her over-tight corset without attracting attention.

"I know a few things—how it's made, how to taste it, how to store it, that sort of thing. But it's not as if I write for the *Wine Spectator*. I'm strictly an amateur."

If she recognized the name of that world famous newsletter for wine collectors and connoisseurs, she pretended otherwise.

"Well, in any event, I think that's wonderful. I never could make head nor tails out of a wine list. My late husband always drank vodka, poor sod."

Hoyt Asbury gave Mrs. Bates a withering glare. "I think its all bloody crap, anyway," he said with a snort. "I read somewhere that if you blindfold someone they can't tell the difference between a good wine and grape juice. All this swirling and swishing and spitting is a lot of poppycock, I say."

"You're absolutely right, Mr. Asbury. Taste depends a lot upon both sight and smell. Without either of those senses to aid us, we might as well be drinking grape juice, as you say. As for wine tasting, I'll admit the ritual looks a bit pretentious—

"Bloody poppycock." Asbury said, punctuating each syllable with a curt nod of his head.

"Mr. Asbury, please," Mrs. Bates said, shaking her head, eyes narrowing in disapproval.

I smiled, noting the older man's discomfort. "Anyway, the tasting process is strictly a means to enhance the pleasure of drinking the wine, nothing more. As for my alleged expertise, if you'll allow me...."

"Far be it from me to impose," Harlan said, handing me the wine list. "It's all yours, kiddo."

I glanced at Maddy, who gave me a reassuring wink.

The first thing I noticed on the list were the modern vintages. I was relieved. Aside from their scarcity, most 1912 wines would be little more than expensive vinegar. It was a minor miracle that the champagne Harlan had given me back in Gdansk had been any good at all, though I'd long suspected he'd taken a far more recently bottled vintage and had it re-labeled.

In all, I ordered five different wines: a Pinot Grigio and a dry Chardonnay for the lighter fish and poultry courses, two vintage Burgundies for the meat dishes: *Chateau Margeaux* and *La Tache Domaine De La Romanée-Conti*, as well as a delightful late harvest Riesling for dessert.

While the Sommelier, returned with the first of the wines, the first course was being served.

"I have a confession to make," Maddy whispered, in between bites of her Oyster á la Russe. I fought back the feeling of dread that stole over me and forced a smile onto my face.

"Nothing bad, I hope." It was a trite thing to say, but because of the way I was feeling at that moment, I couldn't think of anything else. And that earnest look on her face made it all the worse, as did her next words.

"You're going to hate me...."

This was the moment she would tell me she was married.

"I assure you I won't," I said, all the while my stomach roiled.

"I've never read one of your books...until last night."

I was relieved and stunned all at once and my expression must have shown it.

She laughed. "I'm sorry, but you looked so surprised just then. What did you think I was going to say?"

"I don't know, Maddy, but you made it all sound so melodramatic. I had visions of all sorts of wicked things. You worried me."

She rested her hand on mine, infusing me with her warmth. "You're such a dear man."

I shook my head. "Oh, God, don't say that. The next thing you'll say is that I'm 'such a nice guy.' And after that we'll just be friends."

I couldn't believe I'd said that. But instead of acting indignant, as I would have expected, she merely smiled one of her sly smiles. "Oh, I don't think we'll ever be *just* friends, Trevor."

Back from a short break, the band began playing. Consisting of an octet of stringed instruments, they sat in the open area just inside the double doors, off to the side and played mostly ragtime and other light pieces. When they began a slower tune, a waltz from *The Merry Widow*, Maddy turned to me. "Dance with me, Galahad?"

"I don't think they allow that. What I mean is, I don't think they did that on the original ship, at least not in the dining room."

"Go on, Trev, enjoy yourself," Harlan said.

"But no one else is doing it."

"Trevor," Maddy said, disappointed. "Don't you *want* to dance with me?"

"More than anything. The trouble is...I never learned how."

She stood and held out her hand to me. "No time like the present. I promise not to lead you astray."

"And I promise not to turn your feet into hamburger," I replied, taking her hand.

She led the way to the area right in front of the band. The leader, the violinist, smiled and gave us an encouraging nod. Maddy took me in her arms and pulled me to her. She felt soft and delicate, yet underneath I sensed a hard core, a toughness I admired. She was the kind of person who would meet a challenge head on, rather than shy away as so many others would. I admired that quality, and wished I had more of it within me. Sometimes, being a writer allowed me to indulge the part of me that wanted to hide from the world, and I was beginning to chafe under that regime.

"You know, you might do a lot better if you moved," Maddy said.

"What? Oh, I'm sorry." I leaned close to her and whispered in her ear. "What the hell do I do?"

"Just go with the flow," she whispered back.

We began to sway to the lilting rhythms and I suddenly found it easy to dance with her. When I was a young boy, my mother had forced dancing lessons on me. After a while, I ducked them, spending the time in a local pool hall that didn't mind a bored and curious kid hanging around. Right now, I really wished I'd gone more often.

"How am I doing?"

Her smile dazzled me. "Just fine, Galahad, just fine."

I leaned closer and heard her sigh. Her hair smelled of honeysuckle and that rush of giddiness returned.

"So, uhh, what did you think of my book? I assume you got it from the ship's library."

"They have all of them, so I picked the very first one."

"It's my favorite. It was rejected over thirty times before it got published, and I thought if I had to rewrite it one more time, I would jump out my window."

"I'm glad you didn't."

"Me, too."

The music ended and the band struck up a fast ragtime. Since neither one of us knew what to do with that kind of music, we returned to the table and our soup course.

Two hours later, the meal finally wound down. I'd managed to stick to my plan to eat sparingly of each course, savoring it for its unique flavor. The others, excluding Harlan and Maddy who'd followed my lead, appeared dazed and logy.

Harlan broke the momentary silence. "If you gentlemen would care to join me in the smoking room for cigars and port, I would be honored." He turned to Maddy. "Ladies, if you will excuse us."

Maddy looked at me and I knew what she was thinking.

"Harlan, if you don't mind, Maddy and I are going to take a turn around the deck."

He smiled, this time without any conspiratorial overtones. "Of course. I'll see you later." Then to the others. "Gentlemen, let us retire."

Hoyt struggled to his feet and was joined by Gavin Reynolds who looked even thinner standing up. The three of them joined a growing throng of men headed for the smoking room one deck above.

"Are you sure you don't want to join them?" Maddy said.

Though her question was innocent, I could discern the true subtext. I shook my head, helping her on with her wrap. "No thanks. I never could stand to be in a smoky room. Besides, I'd have to be crazy to leave you alone."

She laughed, and together we walked out of the Dining Saloon, taking a lift up to the Boat deck.

Outside, the temperature had dropped and she huddled next to me, her arm around my waist. We walked the length of the deck at a leisurely pace, passing a few of our fellow passengers on similar missions.

The moon was a hemisphere of silver hanging overhead, and the stars stretched from horizon to horizon like a brilliant pointillist tapestry.

"It's beautiful, isn't it?" Maddy said, staring upward, the pale light making the ivory pallor of her skin glow. "You forget when you live in a city, just how breathtaking the night sky really is. I'll bet it looked just this way a hundred years ago...."

I stared at her until my silence made her turn. "What is it?" she said, a smile playing across her lips.

"Who are you, Maddy Regehr?"

"Isn't this where you're supposed to say, 'Where have you been all my life?'"

"That was on my mind, too, but I realized, just now actually, that you know all about me, and I know next to nothing about you."

"You're not trying for one of your interviews."

"No, I'm not. But so what if I were? Is your life story that bad?"

A troubled look flashed across her face, revealing fine lines I'd never seen, lines that didn't belong on this woman's countenance, lines of unhappiness.

"I really don't want to talk about it, Trevor. Can we change the subject?"

The writer in me, the one who wanted to ferret out the truth, urged me to press on; but I knew that to do so would alienate her from me, possibly for good. And I couldn't do that, for I knew that whatever it is we felt for each other was still on tenuous ground.

"Isn't that your friend?" she asked, motioning toward the stern with a nod of her head.

I followed her gaze and saw Harlan down on the Poop Deck striding past the docking bridge on his way toward the aftermost point. He appeared to be in a hurry. I frowned.

"You mind if we go down there?"

"You're worried about him, aren't you?"

"Is it that obvious?"

She nodded. "Yes, it is. Are you sure you want to get involved?"

She had my attention now.

"Why would you say that?"

"No reason, except that all of us have our secrets, and sometimes it's best if we don't plumb too deep."

"That go for you, too?"

She remained silent, a beautiful, maddening enigma more enticing by the moment.

"Come on, let's go."

Except for two men having an argument about sports statistics, the Poop Deck lay mostly deserted. We found Harlan leaning on the railing looking out over the ship's wake. It took him a few minutes to realize we were there and until he did, he seemed forlorn, an expression I'd never seen on him before.

"Wasn't the food terrific, Trev?" he asked, without turning around. "Can you believe people really ate like that, and lived long and healthy lives? And now look at us." He turned and fixed me with an angry glare. "We're all running scared, worried about every miserable thing we put into our bodies." He shook his head, and I took it as my cue to voice concerns that had gnawed at me since the voyage began.

"Is everything all right, Harlan?"

He gave me an odd look, then smiled. "Sure, kiddo, everything's fine. At any rate, it's nothing a sea voyage won't cure."

I saw a look pass between him and Maddy, and I felt a flash of white-hot jealousy.

"So, how are you two getting along?" he said, the smile returning. "It isn't often I get to play the *yenta*."

I looked to Maddy, whose expression was unreadable.

"Not that I'm complaining, Harlan, but you've never been so inclined in the past, certainly not when we were at Harvard together. Why now? And how do you two know each other, anyway?"

He laughed, and turned to Maddy. "Now, you see why I invited him. He's going to write a hell of a book. Knows just the right questions to ask."

"So, how about answering them?" I said.

"Which one?"

He was toying with me, evading the questions, perhaps because of a prior relationship with Maddy. And even as the anger rose within me, I knew it was crap. I'd known Maddy for mere hours, and yet I knew—with an instinctive certainty—that she wasn't the type who would let an old boyfriend fix her up with a new one. Unless, of course, it was all part of some sick joke. I shoved that ugly thought from my mind. It was unworthy of both of them. Still, the doubts lingered.

I was about to restate my questions when Harlan laughed. "I'm sorry, kiddo, too much wine tonight. I've only known Maddy since the news broke about the ship. She was one of many applicants I personally interviewed, and she impressed me with her *joie de vivre*, and her artistic nature. I thought the two of you would hit it off. Nothing mysterious."

Now, it was my turn to laugh.

"What are you talking about? Your whole method for peopling this ship is mysterious."

Harlan shrugged, and I chalked it up to another one of his rich-man's idiosyncracies. Lord knew he had plenty; I was standing on one. I sensed Maddy's impatience growing, and so I bid him goodnight. We resumed our stroll, this time along the port side, and it was a long time before we spoke.

"What are you thinking?" she said, finally breaking the silence.

I halted in my tracks, turning her to face me. "I'm thinking that I must be losing my mind. First, I let Harlan sweep me off my feet with his improbable dream to rebuild the *Titanic*, then I rushed through the revisions of my new novel, so I could write a book about it, a book I'm now having doubts about, and now I find myself falling in love with a woman I've just met, who won't even tell me the least bit about herself. So, what do you think? Am I nuts?"

Her eyes went wide as saucers.

"What did you say?"

"I said, I think I'm falling in love—"

She lunged into my arms, pressing her lips against mine with desperate frenzy. I responded in kind, pulling her to my body, eliciting a sharp moan from deep within her throat. She clutched my back, nails digging into the fabric of my evening clothes. I grew dizzy, drunk with a passion that left me trembling, and the world spinning around me. Aroused beyond any moment I'd ever known, I reacted with instinct and reached for her breasts.

"NO!" she screamed, pulling away from me, her arms wrapping around herself protectively. She moved toward the railing, her breath coming in short gasps.

I was both alarmed at her reaction and ashamed that I'd caused it, wondering if perhaps she was the victim of an assault. But she didn't fit the psychological profile, at least not according to the one Julia had often quoted: *that assault victims inevitably withdraw into themselves.*

If anything Maddy was too outgoing. Could that be the sign of a different paradigm? As a writer it sounded plausible, but as a man on the verge of hopeless love, it was an idea my heart had to reject.

Another moment passed and I saw her steady herself. I moved to the railing.

"Maddy, I'm sorry, I didn't mean to hurt you. I got carried away. Can you forgive me?"

She shook her head, and when she spoke, it was as if she hadn't heard me, caught up in some distant fugue within herself. "This was a bad idea, a very bad idea. God, what was I thinking!" She turned to me, her emerald eyes piercing the dark with an intensity that rocked me. "Trevor, I want you to know that you're a sweet, wonderful man, and any woman would be lucky to have you.... But this can't work. I'm sorry...."

She burst into tears and ran off down the promenade, disappearing through the door leading to the forward Grand Staircase. I stood rooted to the spot, stunned into immobility, my heart on the verge of shattering. To have come so close to that which so many aspire and so few attain, only to have it snatched away, was unbearable.

I fought back my emotions and the urge to run after her, knowing it would be a fool's errand. Whatever it was that haunted her, I knew it was a demon she would never subdue alone. I only hoped she would come to see that we could destroy it together. If not...?

I had no answer for that question, at least not one I wished to confront alone on that dark cold night in the North Atlantic. And while I knew the coming of the dawn would find my feelings for her stronger than ever, I could only pray that Maddy would feel the same way.

WEDNESDAY
APRIL 11, 2012

9

I awoke before dawn broke and tried to write an opening to the new book. I sat in my silk dressing gown, the light emanating from my laptop the only illumination in the room. I was having little success. Aside from the fact that nothing I wrote inspired me, I was haunted by what had happened with Maddy on the Boat deck. She'd even invaded my dreams, my waking time disturbed by vague feelings and images I could no longer clearly recall.

Outside, the sky had turned gray, the stars winking out one by one, signaling the inevitability of the new day. I had to find a hook for the narrative, or I was afraid the project would never come together. Oh, the public would love the back story: how Harlan had announced his intentions to rebuild the *Titanic* with such flair and drama. And I fully intended to infuse the story of the ship's construction with as much of that as possible.

But the fact remained that the story lacked a heart. I still needed to find it. The captain's interview, while affecting, was only one such story. There were others on board, equally moving, and I needed to hear them, to find out why *they* were here. Even as I typed, one thought kept running around in my head: *I loved Maddy.*

As crazy as that sounded, I was as sure of it as I could be of anything; and I wanted her to feel that way about me—needed it, in fact. But as my agent always so eloquently put it, "it was time to screw the muse."

I had to stop moping around and get to work. Maybe then, I could deal with Maddy without losing myself in the process.

The sun had just crept over the distant horizon when a soft, insistent knock came at the door.

"Come in, Henry," I said, without looking up from the screen.

He bustled in pushing a cart ladened with an enormous breakfast, consisting of Eggs Benedict smothered in Hollandaise sauce, a rasher of bacon that looked as if it were half the pig, kippers, toast with marmalade, milk, orange juice, and a silver pot filled with steaming coffee.

"I hope you're joining me, Henry," I said, enjoying his nonplused reaction.

"Sir?"

"Surely you don't expect me to eat all of this myself?"

"It wouldn't be seemly, sir."

"Seemly? For Christ's sake, this isn't 1912, or did Harlan instruct you to behave as if it were?"

"Nothing of the kind, sir. Mr. Astor never mentioned any acting as part of my job."

I poured myself a cup of the coffee and grabbed a piece of toast, slathering some marmalade on it. "You could have fooled me, Henry. You're playing the part to the hilt. Probably get an Oscar, or whatever it is they hand out to menservants."

The arching of his eyebrows was the only comment on my lame attempt at wit. He then turned his attention to my laptop, now displaying my custom screen saver. It showed a miniature *Titanic* sailing back and forth across the screen.

"I see you've begun, sir. Bravo."

"Maybe you'd better save your bravos, for the moment."

He bent over the cart and began preparing a plate. I watched him out of the corner of my eye, while he piled on the food, curious to see if it was for him or me.

"Going badly, sir?"

"The muse is a fickle lady. Sometimes she's not so cooperative. Right now, she's downright ornery, I'd say."

"What is it you're trying to say?"

I turned and looked at him. This had gone well beyond the idle banter between servant and (*I hated to use the word*) master. He seemed genuinely interested. So, I told him about what I had in mind: combining interviews with my own perspective. And I had to hand it to him, he listened. Unlike most people. When I was finished, he handed me the plate and offered his opinion in a straightforward, no-nonsense manner.

"If I were you, sir, I would stay the course you're on. It's a sound idea. After the voyage is over, I'm sure the public will be clamoring to know more...." He replaced the covers on the platters of food. "What are you calling the book, if I may be so bold?"

I hesitated a moment, unsure if I wanted to voice it at this point. Call me superstitious, or whatever, but I liked to keep the titles of my books secret until the last possible moment. However, for some unfathomable reason, I decided to reveal it. Perhaps it was Henry's unflappable nature that prompted me, or maybe I just plain trusted him.

"*Titanic 2012*," I replied, a little self-conscious.

The older man nodded, rolling it around in his mind. "Very good, sir. Quite commercial."

"Thank you, Henry, I'm glad you think so. And you've been a great help, by the way."

"You're quite welcome, sir," he said.

All of a sudden, my stomach growled and I realized I was ravenous. I attacked the plate of food with gusto, relishing every bite. By drawing me out, Henry had known I would be hungry and had gone about fixing up my plate all the while he was assuaging my doubts. Julia could learn a thing or two from such a man.

And then another thought hit me. "Henry? What about you? I'll bet you have a lot of interesting stories to tell."

He'd been making my bed and straightened up when I proposed making him a part of the book.

"That would be quite impossible, sir. One never speaks of one's employers."

"Oh, I didn't mean that. I meant your life in general."

"Exactly, sir," he said with bow.

Chastened, I resumed eating, not knowing quite what to make of what he'd just said. To have immersed oneself so totally into one's profession that one *became it* was an astounding concept. And perhaps a little sad in Henry's case.

Then again, all I had to do was look in the mirror. What was I, if not a writer? It was not simply what I did; it was a vital part of me. As much as I might want to see further into this elegant, enigmatic man, he'd erected an impenetrable barrier, one I had to respect.

Henry tidied up the stateroom and left with the breakfast dishes twenty minutes later, at least I thought it was twenty minutes. His insightful advice had given me back my confidence, and I assaulted the keyboard with abandon. An hour later, I had the first drafts of both the introduction and the first chapter completed.

Feeling a sense of satisfaction I hadn't felt since coming aboard *Titanic*, I closed up my laptop, grabbed my DVD recorder and my windbreaker and left the suite. It was time to find another subject to interview.

The day was mild for the Irish Sea at that time of year, the warmth of the sun bringing out throngs of my fellow travelers, who strolled the deck or lounged on the wooden deck chairs, their noses buried in the latest best sellers. I even noticed one fellow reading a paperback edition of my last Conrad Holm novel.

Seeing them now raised my spirits, even as I noticed yet one more odd thing about the voyage: *there were no children aboard.* Ages ranged from the elderly to those in their mid-teens. And the lack of couples that I'd observed earlier still seemed to be the case. Oh, there were those who *looked* as if they were paired off, but they exuded none of the intense vibrations one got from those passionately in love.

These thoughts compelled me to search for Maddy, but the crowds were too thick. On impulse, I tried the bow in the hopes that she would again be there, spreading her arms to the sun; however, this time, my intuition failed me.

Instead, I spotted a teenaged girl and boy acting out that famous scene. I smiled, a deep longing filling me. Perhaps I was wrong about there being no couples on board, at least I hoped I was. Not only for them, but for me, as well.

I found my next subject standing on the Boat deck gazing out over the ocean, her expression serene. She appeared to be in her early forties, dressed in an expensive pant suit, with dark brown hair and a pleasant girl-next-door face. She looked exceedingly average, which is what attracted me to her.

"Excuse me, but do you mind if I ask you some questions?"

She turned to me, her brows furrowed in puzzlement. "Oh, I'm sorry, what did you say? I was daydreaming. I do far too much of that these days." She smiled, and I found myself liking her at once.

"I'm sorry, I didn't mean to bother you, but I was wondering if I could ask you a few questions for a book I'm doing about the voyage."

"Really? I guess that would be okay. But you're going to be bored, I assure you, Mr...."

"Please, forgive me," I said, pulling out my DVD recorder. "I'm Trevor Hughes."

She stuck out her hand. "Jenny Powell. Do you want to do it here, or do we go somewhere else?"

I pointed to one of the wood-and-cast-iron benches a few feet away. "How about over there?"

"That's fine. I can still see the ocean that way. I never get tired of looking at it. Do you, Mr. Hughes?"

I took a seat on the bench and placed the recorder between us. "Call me, Trevor," I said. "And, no, I never do...."

10

Interview with Jenny Powell
Location: Boat Deck

W hat should I say?"
"Anything you want; mostly I'd like to know why you wanted to sail on the *Titanic*."

She nodded, looking down at her hands for a long moment. Then she raised her eyes to me. "My name's Jenny, I'm forty-two years old, I was married once for five months, was truly in love only once, and I work in the main branch of a major bank in New York. Oh, and I'm dying...."

My throat went dry at those last words, and I resisted the urge to speak. She didn't look like the type who needed prompting, anyway.

"I guess you could say my life was pretty boring— didn't I say that before? Anyway, I was raised in the Midwest, had four brothers and three sisters, who were always fighting with each other, and parents more concerned with being righteous than with loving us.

"They were Jehovah's Witnesses, you see. Half our lives were spent on the road handing out tracts printed on cheap paper with ink that rubbed off on your hands. That's the thing I remember the most about my childhood. Hands with black palms...and slamming doors.

"As soon as I was old enough, I moved away. I even changed my name, did it legal and proper, because I wanted nothing from them, not even their name. I wanted a fresh start."

"How old were you?" I asked.

"Eighteen. And as wet behind the ears as one could be at that age. But I'd saved enough money over the years from summer jobs to rent a cheap studio apartment in San Francisco. I had aspirations, you see. I wanted to be an artist. The problem was I had more romantic notions than talent, and ended up squandering what cash I had. And because I didn't finish school no one would hire me."

"What did you do?"

She shook her head sadly. "What a lot of girls do: I got married as fast as I could. Paulo was a young art student whose rich father subsidized him. He was dark and handsome, and somewhat charming when he wasn't drinking White Russians. He thought that was an artist's drink, you see.

"We met in a little coffee house in the Haight where they hung his canvasses and read bad poetry out loud. One thing I had to admit, though, he could really paint."

"What school?"

"I guess you'd call it 'photo-realism.' The stuff he did was uncanny. It looked so real that you'd swear it was a photograph. And the illusion would maintain its integrity until you got right up close and could then see his brush strokes. His secret, he said, was in thinning the paint to the right degree and using small brushes, sometimes as fine as one hair. Anyway, he saw me staring at one of his paintings and he introduced himself. He said I looked intelligent, that I could sense the underlying truth of things. I told him he was full of shit." Jenny smiled. "He laughed, and then asked me if I would pose for him. Nude, of course.

"I see the question in your eyes. Yes, I did pose for him, and it turned out to be one of the very best things he'd ever done. In a way, he'd made me look better than I did in real life. In the process, we fell in love and were married two months later, a big Catholic ceremony with all of his family in attendance. Mine were no shows, of course. You see, Jehovah's Witnesses don't believe in celebrating any holidays or special occasions, not even birthdays.

"The first month was heaven, and then things fell apart. He began seeing other women almost at once, and he didn't even try to hide it. I think he considered it his right as a man, or some such crock. The day I caught him in bed with twins I moved out. I hocked the engagement ring, which gave me enough to move to L.A. and start again. I got a job in a bank and worked my way up to Vice President. By the time I was thirty-five, I was making a good living. But I was lonely. I don't know, maybe being a workaholic was my way of avoiding the Paolos of the world, but I finally realized that I was punishing *myself*, not him. So, I decided to do something about it."

"And what was that?" I said, more and more intrigued with her story.

"My friends set me up with blind dates. And God, were those disasters. All of them were either preening self-absorbed types who felt they were doing you a favor, or crushing bores who talked ceaselessly about their careers. I also tried the video dating thing and various singles organizations. But they were the proverbial meat markets. I finally gave up, deciding to quit while I was behind. You know that old saying: *You'll find what you're looking for when you stop looking for it?* Well, its true.

"I got a flyer in the mail about a poetry reading at the library. I still get goose bumps when I think about this because I really feel that fate took a hand, somehow. Instead of throwing it out, I read it and decided to go as a lark. It certainly wasn't what I expected, to say the least. It turned out to be a *lesbian* poetry reading, and when I realized it, I waited for an opportunity to leave. And then, Nina got up to read and my whole world turned upside-down.

"I'd never been attracted to women before, at least not on a conscious level, but her poetry spoke to my heart in ways that Paolo never could. After the reading, I made my way up to her, stomach all twisted up in knots. She was surrounded by all these butch types, and she was like this feminine flower, all aglow. I was so nervous that I could barely speak, but when our eyes met, I knew—I just knew my search was over...and so was hers.

"You asked me why I wanted to sail on the *Titanic*. Well, a part of the reason probably won't surprise you. On our first date we went to see a re-release of the director's cut, the one with the extra twenty minutes. We'd both loved the film ever since we'd first seen it as kids. My parents thought it was an abomination, of course. Anyway, you remember the line Rose says to Jack at the end when the ship's about to sink: 'You jump, I jump, right?' Well, that was Nina and me to a tee. We moved in together a few days later and spent seven beautiful years together...." Jenny's eyes welled up with tears, and I handed her my handkerchief. "Thank you," she said, dabbing her eyes.

I waited until she had regained her composure, then pressed on. "So, what happened with you and Nina?"

"Not what you think. We were happy. Oh, we had our moments, fights over the usual stupid things couples argue about, and some serious things, too. Like taking me to meet her parents, you know."

I nodded, reassuring.

"Nina was a wonderful person, but so damned insecure. One thing she always said was that she never wanted to live without me. I was touched by that, at first, but it got to be a little weird, too. And then, last year, it all came crashing down. That was when I was diagnosed with cancer of the lymph nodes. Nina went off the deep end, started talking about a suicide pact. She even bought these pills from some survivalist wacko, said they were cyanide, and kept them locked in her jewelry case.

"Well, I forgot about them, didn't really believe her, anyway. Besides, I was fighting for my life. I *wanted* to live. I went through the chemo and the radiation, and for awhile it seemed to be working. But, Nina instinctively knew what I was denying even to myself: that the war was already lost. I found her in the apartment on a lazy Friday afternoon. She was supposed to meet me at our favorite little bistro. I'd waited for over an hour before my alarm bells compelled me to go home. She was lying on the bed, perfectly composed, the note lying next to her head. My vision was so blurred with tears and my hands shook so much that I could barely read it. It said: *'I couldn't wait any longer, lover. I jump, you jump, right? See you soon.'* That was it! See you soon. As if we were due to have lunch next week. Oh, God!"

Jenny broke down at that point and I took her in my arms and held her while she sobbed against me. And I'm not ashamed to say that I cried, too. Her story had touched the very core of me. After five minutes, she calmed down and pulled away.

"I'm okay," she said, wiping her eyes.

"One thing I want to know," I said. "And I'm sorry if this comes off sounding callous and cold: but did she leave a pill for you?"

"Yes. It was right next to her on the bed resting on a little satin pillow, like something out of a dainty magazine ad."

"What did you do with it?"

"I still have it, though I don't think I could ever use it. Not that I'm afraid, you understand, it's just that every time I look at it, I see her lying there, the tiniest of smiles on her face. I wanted her to *live* with me, dammit! Instead, she chose to abandon me."

"And you can't forgive her for that?"

"I can, and I have," she said, meeting my gaze. "I just can't forgive myself."

"For what?"

"For not seeing that she didn't have the strength to fight the disease with me. It's ironic, isn't it? I get sick, and she dies." Jenny fell silent for a long moment. "Can we stop now? I'm feeling a bit tired."

"Sure, no problem. You've been very kind to speak with me."

"Am I going to be in your book?"

"Only if you want to be."

"I do." Jenny nodded, her expression one of firm resolve. "Maybe I can help someone else. I mean, there might be an afterlife, and I'd like to think I'll see Nina again, but a part of me resists that. I guess I'm still rebelling against my parents, huh? Anyway, if I could tell the world one thing it would be to enjoy what you've got before it slips away and all you're left with are your regrets...."

11

After I was sure she would be all right, I left Jenny on the Boat Deck, and proceeded to the Marconi Room. Sammy was on duty, and he smiled and waved to me with one hand, while the other busily scribbled the translation of an incoming message. A few minutes later, he put down his pencil ripped the message off his pad and placed it into his "out" box, then tore off his headphones with a sigh.

"Bloody long one that," he said, rubbing his ears, fiery red from having to wear the headset for hours at a stretch.

"Anything good?" My question was meant to be facetious; Sammy took it at face value.

"Someone's idea of a joke, sending me an ice warning from the bloody *Baltic*. Aside from the fact that particular ship hasn't existed for ninety years, icebergs are lot fewer and farther between than they used to be. Talk was last year they were even going to disband the I.I.P."

He was talking about the International Ice Patrol, organized by England and the United States in the wake of the *Titanic* disaster.

"Of course it's all satellite-based now, so there's not much else to do but look at a bloomin' computer screen." He then shook his head and shrugged. "Anyway, I suppose you've got another one of your dispatches?"

"If it's not too much trouble."

"No trouble at all, mate. It'll be right enjoyable compared to what I've been doing. Have a seat."

I'd culled some of what was now the book's first chapter and I dictated it to Sammy. I watched his face as he keyed the words, and his normally placid expression became animated. When we finished, he turned to me.

"That from your book?"

I nodded, putting away my notes. "Part of the first chapter."

"Well, if the rest of it's as good as that, you'll have a right best seller."

"Thanks. I'll send you an autographed copy."

"You don't have to do that," he said, suddenly distracted.

"Maybe not, but I want to."

Sammy nodded, adjusting his headphones. "Send it round to me Mum. She'll be wanting one, for sure."

"My pleasure."

The Marconi began clicking, signaling that another message was arriving, and I took that as my cue to leave. I was wrung out from Jenny's story and from my less than restful sleep the night before. Still, I was troubled by what had happened with Maddy and I wanted to confront her, to find out what had caused such an emotional about-face, maybe help her get past it, if possible. Of course my motives were not completely unselfish. I wanted to be in the safe haven of her arms once more.

My first stop was the Purser's Office, situated amidship on C-deck. I came up to the window and spotted the Purser seated at his tiny desk poring over a ledger. He looked up at me, his hawkish face registering surprise. "Oh, I'm sorry, sir," he said, unfolding his tall, lanky frame out of his chair. "I didn't see you. What can I do for you?"

"I was wondering if you could help me locate a fellow passenger. She's in steerage somewhere, and forgot to tell me which room she's in."

The Purser smiled and pulled a clipboard off a hook on the wall. "Certainly, sir. What is the lady's name?"

"Madeleine Regehr."

He ran his long index finger down the page, his brow furrowed in thought. I noticed most of his knuckles were swollen with arthritis.

"Ahh, here it is," he said, turning the clipboard, so I could read it. "Right here."

It was a berth number located somewhere on E-deck in the forecastle. The man was kind enough to point it out on a floor plan mounted to the wall behind him. I thanked him and headed off.

Even with his clear, concise directions, it took me far longer to find her room than it should have. Third class reminded me of a topiary maze I'd gotten lost in as a child: corridors branching off into more corridors, all of them looking alike. I'd circled back to the same point twice before taking the correct turn that brought me to her door.

I felt giddy, lightheaded, and butterflies ceaselessly chased each other inside my intestinal tract. I swallowed my fear and knocked.

Silence.

"Maddy, are you there?"

Again, nothing.

I was annoyed, imagining her sitting there deliberately ignoring me, and I was so wrapped up in my emotional turmoil that it didn't occur to me that she might simply be out.

I pounded on the door, harder, the sound echoing down the lonely corridor.

"Maddy, I'm sorry for what happened, please open up."

The door to the room next to hers swung open and a bleary-eyed man with thick black stubble on his chin and a scowl on his face leaned out.

"What the bloody hell is going on here?"

"I'm sorry for disturbing you, but I'm looking for the woman who's staying here."

The man rolled his eyes.

"Cor blimey! That bloody flake moved out early this morning! And bloody good riddance to 'er. Crying and playing the same bloody love songs on her warbler over and over all night, she was."

Hearing that she'd had a rough night aroused mixed feelings in me. A part of me was the tiniest bit glad that she'd suffered long after leaving me standing on the promenade. The other part of me felt as if a white-hot lance had pierced my solar plexus. But all of that was immediately overshadowed when I remembered her telling me about working her way up to first class. Feeling more than a little foolish, I started back down the hall.

"Sorry, to have bothered you," I said, calling back over my shoulder.

The man mumbled something I couldn't make out, shook his head and disappeared back into his room.

I ran back the way I'd come, passing the lowermost First Class staterooms on E-deck. Second Class staterooms were farther aft and confined to the starboard side. I kept my eyes peeled for a steward and was soon rewarded: one was exiting one of the last of the First Class staterooms when I approached.

"Excuse me, but I was wondering if you could help me locate someone?"

The steward looked to be about eighteen, but a closer examination of his boyish face revealed a fine web of crow's feet spreading out from the corners of his eyes, as well as a smattering of gray at his temples.

"Have you tried the Purser's Office?" he asked in a pleasant voice tinged with a public school accent.

I told him about Maddy's intention to move around on the mostly-empty ship, and the steward frowned.

"That is a bit of a problem. What does she look like?"

I described her as thoroughly as possible, and when I got to her auburn hair, his smile returned. "I saw her, not more than half an hour ago."

"Thank you so much," I said, relieved. "Did she seem okay?"

"How do you mean, sir?"

"Did she seem upset, agitated?"

"Not that I noticed but, then again, I was a trifle busy at the time."

"I know this is asking a lot, but do you remember the stateroom number?"

The steward shook his head. "I'm sorry, sir, I don't. But I could show it to you."

I followed him down the corridor and a moment later he stopped in front of a stateroom marked: E-75. He knocked on the door and we both waited, listening for a response. He tried once more, then turned to me. "I'm sorry, sir, but it seems the lady is out."

"Thank you, anyway, you've been most helpful."

"My pleasure, sir.... After all, courtesy and civility are all we have left."

I looked at him, puzzled. "What do you mean?"

Now, it was his turn to look puzzled, and then a little nervous. "I'm sorry, sir, I guess I'm just bemoaning the state of modern society. If you'll excuse me, I must get back to work. So glad to have been of help."

He marched back down the corridor and I watched him go, feeling a vague sense of disquiet. Courtesy and civility were certainly casualties of the modern age, but were they really all we had left? I certainly hoped not, or we were all in big trouble.

Checking my watch, I realized that it was nearly lunch time, and would be a logical reason for Maddy not to be in her stateroom. We were also due into Cobh. I located the lifts and took one up to D-deck.

The dining saloon was already busy, and it took me a moment to locate her. She was seated at a table for two near one of the windows, studying the menu. The sun streamed through the glass, glinting off the highlights in her auburn hair, making them burn like tiny flames. Her expression was so calm, so placid that I began to wonder if she'd really suffered as the bleary-eyed man in steerage had purported.

Realizing that I made an odd picture standing as I was in the middle of the saloon floor, I pushed all doubts from my mind and closed the distance between us. She didn't see me until I was right in front of her.

Her smile was tinged with sadness and regret, yet I also detected a hopeful quality, which buoyed my spirits beyond measure. Perhaps the situation was not as bleak as it seemed.

"Hi, Maddy.... Are you okay?"

She nodded. "I'm better, thanks," she said. "Would you like to sit down?"

She indicated the seat opposite her own, and I slid into it, grateful that the unpleasant scene I'd anticipated had not materialized. And though I was ecstatic to be with her, I restrained myself. Something inside me, call it the voice of bitter experience, told me to play it cool. An awkward moment passed, while she toyed with the swizzle stick of her Gimlet, eyes downcast.

"I want to apologize for what happened, Trevor," she said, finally meeting my gaze. "I acted like a silly schoolgirl. Can you forgive me?"

"Of course I can," I said. "If you can forgive me."

She frowned, puzzled. "For what? You didn't do anything wrong."

"Then what happened, Maddy? Why'd you act like that?"

We were interrupted by a steward approaching the table to take my drink order. "Would you like some wine?" I asked her. She nodded, distracted by something outside our window. I turned to the steward. "Robert Mondavi, *Coastal*, 1996."

"Very good, sir," he said. A moment later the steward turned and left, and I leaned closer to Maddy, catching a whiff of her subtle perfume. "What happened? Tell me."

She reached across the table and took my hand in hers. "I guess you took me by surprise when you said you were falling in love with me."

"And I'd say you amply returned the favor when you kissed me. That still doesn't explain why you ran off like that."

The wine came at that moment, and I sat back with growing impatience while the steward opened the bottle. For once I found the whole ritual excruciating.

I waved away the cork and bade him to fill both glasses, relieved when he finally left the table. I estimated that we had perhaps five minutes before the steward returned to take our food orders. She sipped her wine and I could tell she was reticent to continue.

"Maddy, if I came on too fast, I'm sorry. I suppose with everything that's gone on, and the romantic mystique inherent with this ship, it didn't seem too out of place to tell you what I was feeling. I forgot that we'd just met. To me it seems as if we've always known each other."

Her hand tightened on mine and she inhaled sharply, her eyes closing. A moment later they opened, focusing their emerald brilliance on me. "I feel the same way, Trevor. Felt it the moment I first saw you at the bow. And that's why I ran. I came on this voyage to put everything behind me. My life had turned to hell, and the last thing I...expected was you."

"You were about to say 'the last thing I *needed*,'right?"

"Two days ago, that's what I *would* have said. Now...I don't know what to think."

She picked up her glass and guzzled half its contents in one swallow. If my feelings were mixed before, they were now totally mired in confusion. She was telling me that she felt the same way I did, yet she wasn't happy about it, and that disturbed me, profoundly. The man in steerage had called her a flake. Could he have been right?

For a split second I considered standing up and walking out, following the advice of the tiny inner voice that always warned me to run from potentially dangerous situations. The problem was that tiny voice had steered me wrong more than once, and I wasn't about to risk losing something good just because it wasn't easy.

"Can we talk about it?"

She shook her head.

"It's not that important, Trevor. I've come to terms with it. Had the whole night to think it through."

A vivid image of her lying on the bed in her tiny claustrophobic room flashed through my mind.

"So what do you want to do?" I asked.

"How about we just pick up from before all this happened. Can we do that?"

"I can, if you can," I said, managing a smile. I decided right then that whatever had caused last night's misunderstanding would not happen again. It was obvious to me that she'd suffered some kind of trauma, perhaps even been assaulted by a man. And if that was the case, it was not only understandable that she would be skittish, but also would be unwilling to talk about it. She'd come on the voyage to cleanse herself. And I had no desire to raise the ghosts of the past with her. I only wanted to point the way to a happier future. And I was convinced that it was a future that would see the two of us together.

The waiter arrived with the first course, a lobster salad, and in spite of all that had gone on, and the tension I was feeling, I was hungry. After a few bites and half a glass of the Mondavi, I felt comfortable enough to risk some innocent conversation.

"I'm curious about what you do for a living, Maddy. If I had to hazard a guess, I'd say you were an artist, maybe a painter or a sculptress."

"You're not far off," she said. "I went to the Parsons School of Design in New York and I had my own business."

"I'm impressed, an interior decorator."

She wagged a slender finger at me, her eyes twinkling with humor. "Shame on you, Mr. Hughes. House painters call themselves 'decorators.' We prefer the term *designer*. It's more prestigious, and more accurate."

"I stand corrected, Ms. Designer."

She giggled, and my heart soared. The happenings of the previous night now seemed even more hazy and unreal.

"So, what kind of designing do you do?"

"Did. Mostly high-end office space. Companies contacted me when they were moving into new quarters and I would work with them to give them a decor that reflected their corporate image."

"Sounds rather stifling, creatively, I mean."

"You'd be surprised," she said, becoming animated, her hands waving in the air in synch with her words. "Unlike residential, where one usually has to deal with a wife who thinks she knows everything better than you, the CEOs I worked with gave me a few parameters and let me run with the ball. It was wonderful experience and terrific fun."

"And they liked what they got?"

Maddy gave me a sly smile. "It got to the point where I had to turn away business. I suppose I could have hired additional staff, but I didn't want the pressures of running a really large business. I liked the hands-on aspect. It's why I got into it to begin with."

"I'll bet being on this ship is especially fun for you."

"You mean because of all the different styles?"

I nodded.

"One of the things I learned at Parsons is that what we know as the Victorian and Edwardian styles are amalgamations of everything that came before them. They were great at stealing a little of this and a little of that and reconstituting those bits and pieces into approximations of their own. This ship is the ultimate expression of that ideal."

"Whoa, hold on," I said, laughing. "What are you talking about?"

Maddy leaned back in her chair, indicating the dining saloon with a sweeping gesture. "This room is what many would call Jacobean, relating to James I of England. And the influence is definitely there, but like the rest of the ship everything's been altered to fit the times, in this case 1912."

"If you had so much fun, Maddy, why'd you stop? Burnout?"

She folded her hands in her lap and sighed.

"Of a sort. Let's just say that I'm no longer suited for it."

I was about to probe further, my curiosity aroused, when our main course arrived: Capon with an orange glaze. I silently thanked whatever deity reigned above that the voyage would be over in less than a week and I could stop eating all this overrich food.

During our meal, the ship had anchored off Cobh, and it was after lunch, during a stroll around the Boat deck, that we spotted a launch heading out from the docks toward us, weaving through the crush of boats filled with sightseers. When it drew closer, I saw a solemn group of men and women gathered near its bow. A moment later, the launch throttled back and pulled up alongside.

"What's going on, Trevor?" Maddy asked.

I didn't answer her right away; instead, I moved toward the wheelhouse. We met Captain Pierce walking out.

"Good afternoon, Mr. Hughes," he said, a gentle smile playing across his face. "I trust you and your lady friend are enjoying the voyage?"

"Very much, sir." I introduced him to Maddy, and he took her hand and kissed it in the continental way. She beamed, enjoying the attention. "By the way, I just saw a launch pull up alongside. I didn't think we were taking on any more passengers."

"We're not," Captain Pierce said. "The Mayor of Cobh wishes to present Mr. Astor with a token of his town's appreciation. The ceremony's due to begin in a few moments in the First Class Lounge. Would you care to accompany me?"

"We'd be delighted," Maddy said.

The captain held out his arm and Maddy took it, shooting me a surreptitious wink when they began walking toward the entrance that would take them to the Grand Staircase. I smiled, and followed.

To my surprise, the First Class lounge was nearly filled to capacity, the other passengers having known what I had not. As for the Mayor and his entourage, they stood near the back, talking animatedly with Harlan. The three of us made right for the group, stopping a few feet short of them. The captain excused himself and went over to them. Harlan took this as his cue.

"Ladies and gentlemen, may I have your attention, please?"

His voice had not been loud, but the room's clamor instantly fell to a murmur.

"I want to thank you all for coming. As you know, we have anchored off the coast of Cobh as a part of our retracing of the *Titanic's* original route. Back in 1912, this was the last stop she made prior to heading for New York...and her rendezvous with destiny.

"As a gesture of goodwill and appreciation, the mayor and a delegation from the town has come aboard to bestow upon us a token of their esteem. Ladies and gentlemen, without further ado, I give you the Mayor of Cobh, Brendan Donahue."

The room filled with polite applause and the Mayor, a heavyset man of medium height with the bright smile of a professional politician, walked up to Harlan bearing a bronze plaque. The Mayor beamed and nodded at the crowd, clearly in his element. When he began to speak the clapping subsided. For me it made little difference, as the man's accent was so thick it made what he said nearly unintelligible. I caught his last few words, where he echoed Harlan's words about "the town's highest esteem," and watched while he shoved the weighty award into Harlan's hands.

The applause erupted and Harlan hoisted the plaque over his head for all to see. On it was a silhouette of the *Titanic* and the dates 1912-

2012. The rest was too small to read from where I was standing, but I got the basic picture. Harlan handed off the plaque to a waiting steward and was about to shake the Mayor's hand, when a second steward blundered through the crowd, his face dark with worry. He went right to Harlan, leaned in and whispered in his ear. Harlan frowned, then motioned for Captain Pierce to join him. The older man strode quickly over and the whispering continued. The captain's expression turned grim and he nodded once, sending the steward on his way.

The noise level in the room had increased in direct proportion to everyone's curiosity. Harlan raised his hand for quiet.

"I regret to inform you that the planned tea and reception for our honored guests is canceled. We will be weighing anchor in ten minutes. An announcement will be made at dinner this evening. Good day."

Harlan stalked off, leaving the Mayor fuming and the rest of us bewildered. I went over to Captain Pierce who was giving orders to one of the bridge officers.

"What's going on, Captain?" I asked.

He turned to me, looking about ten years older than he had a few minutes before. "I'm sorry to say that one of our passengers has passed away."

"My God, who?"

"Mrs. Bates.... Apparently she had a heart attack."

Maddy groaned. "Oh, no, not now."

I shot her a puzzled glance, then returned my attention to the captain, who looked as if he would rather be anywhere other than where he was. And while I felt sadness for Mrs. Bates, who'd been a delightful old lady, this sudden turn of events bothered me for a different reason.

"I don't mean to pry, Captain, but shouldn't we be arranging to offload the body for an autopsy? There must be procedures for this sort of thing."

Captain Pierce looked off in the direction Harlan had disappeared, his mouth tightening with displeasure. "All I can tell you is that Mr. Astor has ordered a burial at sea. Now, if you'll excuse me."

He moved off and I started after him.

"But wait a minute, we're not *at* sea—"

Maddy grabbed my arm. "Let him go, Trevor, he's got a lot on his mind."

I turned to her, the rush of anger dissipating when I saw the look of sadness and gravity in her eyes. I sighed, shaking my head. "I feel terrible about Mrs. Bates. But this isn't right, Maddy."

"You're right, it isn't. But whatever it is you want to do isn't going to bring that old lady back."

"That's not the point—"

"It's exactly the point, Trevor. She's gone. And she was right where she wanted to be when it happened."

"How do you know that?"

She reached up and caressed my face.

"Because I'm exactly where I want to be," she said, coming into my arms. "Will you walk me to my stateroom? I think I'd like to lie down for awhile."

The crowd had thinned to a trickle of people and we took one of the lifts down to E-deck. When we drew in front of her door, she pulled the heavy skeleton key from inside her purse. I took it from her and unlocked the door, pushing it open. While not nearly as austere as the accommodations in steerage, Maddy's second class stateroom was still far more utilitarian than my suite. Still, it boasted two comfortable-looking bunks.

"Are you going to be all right?" I asked, giving her back her key.

She took it and nodded. "I'll be fine. It was just a shock to hear about Mrs. Bates. I liked her. She had a lot of spirit."

"That she did," I said, remembering her puckish behavior at dinner. God, had it only been the night before?

A moment of awkward silence passed between us, a moment fraught with tension of another kind. We both recognized it, I think, and instinctively knew the time was not right.

"Uhh, maybe I'd better go."

Maddy's generous lips curled into one of her sly grins. "Only if you know what's good for you."

"All too well." I leaned down and kissed her. It had none of the desperate urgency from the night before, but was somehow even more erotic. I pulled away from her when I felt a stirring I knew I couldn't act upon.

"What are you going to do until dinner?" she asked.

"I've got some writing to do."

"That's one of the things I love about you. You're dedicated."

"Some would say obsessed. I guess it depends on your perspective. Anyway, I'll see you later."

Another quick peck and she was gone, the door clicking shut in my face. I turned and retraced my steps down the hall, hating myself more with every step. I'd lied to her.

I had no intention of writing anything until I'd spoken with Harlan. And while my guilt mounted, so did my need for the truth.

Five minutes later, I was back on B-deck standing in front of Harlan's suite. This time there was no steward guarding the door. And when I knocked, I half-expected him not to be there, a part of me dreading any sort of confrontation. I was surprised when the door opened and my friend greeted me with a warm smile and a drink in his hand, dressed in a floor-length dressing gown made of brocaded red silk. "Hey, kiddo, come on in."

Harlan's suite was one of the two Parlor Suites renowned for their rococo opulence. Aside from having a spacious sitting room lying between the two large bedrooms, each also boasted a private promenade deck, where one could breakfast in sumptuous seclusion. Richly appointed beyond even the regular First Class suites, they were not referred to as the "Millionaire Suites" for nothing.

Harlan shut the door, glided over to the bar and picked up a lead crystal decanter half-filled with what appeared to be Scotch. "Would you like something?" he asked, picking up a fresh tumbler.

"No thanks."

I watched him refill his glass from the decanter, then pull a bottle of pills from out of a pocket in the dressing gown. He shook one into his palm, shut the bottle and put it away. He saw me watching him out of the corner of his eyes.

"For my nerves," he said, knocking the pill back and taking a swallow of the whiskey.

"Since when have your nerves ever been a problem?"

"Since I became the owner of the world's biggest yacht. You wouldn't believe all the red tape I went through to get this baby back in the water. People think the ocean is a free place, well, it isn't...." He noticed I was still standing and pointed toward an overstuffed chair. "Why don't you have a seat, take a load off?" He then went over and plopped down onto a delicate-looking Louis Quinze sofa, the ice in his drink clinking noisily.

"I won't be here that long, I've got some work to do."

"Well, if I can't tempt you with creature comforts and a stiff drink, what can I do for you?"

"You can tell me about Mrs. Bates."

Harlan's smile disappeared. "Lousy, huh? Her steward found her in her suite. Someone noticed she wasn't at breakfast this morning—"

"No, I don't mean that. I mean, why did we have to leave Cobh so fast?"

Harlan shrugged. "No mystery there. We have a schedule to keep, and I wanted to get rid of that idiot mayor and his entourage."

I looked at him for a moment. "You must think I'm just as dumb. Come on, Harlan, somebody dies, you take care of it, you don't turn tail and run."

Harlan put down his drink on a hand-carved table made from flamed cherry and stood up. "Trev, I've got my reasons."

"I'm sure you do, but if you don't mind, I'd like to know what in the hell they are."

He eyed me with a sober glance. "Christ, kiddo, you sound like one of those bleeding-heart crusader types, the ones you always hated back in school."

"Do I? Well, maybe I've changed. We all have. You used to confide in me."

I saw a flicker of anger and pain flicker across his face, replaced instantly with the old bravado. "All right, but you're going to feel foolish."

"Try me."

"When I was interviewing prospective passengers, Mrs. Bates revealed her heart condition, said it had reached a critical stage, and would I please let her come aboard? What could I do? I knew she might die on the voyage, but the old woman was dying anyway. I wanted to let her have her dream. Is that so bad?"

"Then why the big announcement? Why piss off your guests and get the rest of us to wonder what the big deal was?"

"I guess I overreacted. I'm human, too, Trev, even if I try my best not to be, sometimes." He laughed and took a swig of whiskey.

"Are you really going to bury her at sea? Is that legal?"

Harlan motioned for me to follow him. "I want to show you something."

Inside his bedroom, a study in Georgian elegance, he went to his dresser, pulled open a drawer and removed a strongbox with a combination dial in the center of its lid. With a few twists of the dial he had it open and pulled out a sheaf of papers. "This is Mrs. Bates's will," he said, flipping through the thick document. "I know it seems a bit weird, but like I said, she knew it was touch and go, and wanted to be prepared." He threw it to me, and when I caught it I saw a handwritten codicil on the last page.

"What you're seeing was added by her a few days before sailing. It says that if the worst happened, she wanted to be buried at sea."

Harlan was right, I felt foolish. Who was I to refuse a dying woman's last request. And whom did it really hurt? No one.

"I'm sorry, Harlan, I guess I'm too much of a bleeding-heart crusader."

Harlan grinned. "Stick with me and we'll fix that in no time."

I started for the door, then stopped. "When is the funeral?"

"Sunrise, tomorrow, on the Poop Deck. I'll be announcing it at dinner for those who wish to attend."

"All right, I'll see you then."

I headed back to my suite. Suddenly, I felt very tired, wanting nothing more than a few hours of blissful oblivion. Upon entering the suite, I noticed that Henry had laid out my evening clothes on the bed.

My "boiled shirt" had been cleaned and starched, and the tails had been brushed and pressed. For a fleeting moment, I wondered what Henry did when he wasn't there. Did he sit in the ship's library reading Victorian novels? Did he play whist with the stewards? I shook my head, too tired to think anymore.

Leaving the clothes undisturbed, I opted to lie down on the bed in the adjoining room. The mattress was harder than mine, but my fatigue overcame my discomfort and I fell asleep soon after, my dreams once again filled with vague and disturbing images.

THURSDAY

APRIL 12, 2012

12

"Sir, you need to wake up!"

I heard Henry's voice as if through a layer of cotton in my ears. Then he must have shaken me, for I bolted awake, sitting up in bed semi-alert. "What's wrong, what's wrong?"

Henry stood a few feet from the bed, looking somewhat sheepish. "So sorry to bother you, sir, but its time for the funeral."

I shook the remaining sleep from my fogged brain. "What? Funeral? That's tomorrow morning."

"Yes, sir, it's six o'clock—a.m." His eyebrow arched in mild disapproval.

Leaping from the bed, I ran over to the window and yanked aside the heavy curtain. The sun hit me square in the face. It should have been *behind* the boat, not in front. Somehow, I'd slept through dinner and right on through the night. And then I remembered Maddy. "Oh, no...."

"Is everything all right, sir?"

I dropped the curtain, cutting off the sunlight and crossed the stateroom, shaking my head. "No, everything's lousy. I was supposed to meet someone for dinner. She probably thinks I'm a jerk."

Henry began tidying the bed, making precise hospital corners out of the twisted mess I'd made from the sheets. "Oh, I wouldn't say so, sir. She quite understood when I told her you were still asleep."

"Wait a minute. She was here? When?"

"About seven-thirty last night, right before dinner."

"Henry, why didn't you wake me? I only wanted to take a short nap."

"I was about to, sir. It was the lady who stopped me. Had I known—"

I cut him off with a wave of my hand. "No, it's okay. You had no way of knowing."

"If I may be so bold, sir, she is quite the catch."

"Thanks, although I seem to be fumbling at the moment."

Henry smoothed over the brocaded coverlet and then went to lay out my clothes for the day. "I don't believe so, sir. She seems quite taken with you."

I followed him into the dressing area, my curiosity aroused. "She did?"

"Oh, yes, sir. She told me to tell you...now, what was it?"

He frowned, his lips pursing while he tried to recall Maddy's words. I had to restrain myself, wanting to shake them out of him.

"Oh, yes," he said, smiling. "She said, 'Tell Galahad that if he knows what's good for him, he'll meet me on the Boat Deck at six-fifteen.'" Henry glanced at his watch and nodded. "By my reckoning, sir, you have about ten minutes."

At that moment, all argument ceased. Working as a team, Henry and I had me dressed and ready to meet the day in slightly under five minutes. I grabbed my DVD recorder and headed out of the suite toward the stairs. Two minutes later, I was up on the Boat deck.

It was moderately crowded, with groups of sober-eyed passengers marching past me on their way toward the Poop deck and Mrs. Bates's impromptu funeral.

I found Maddy standing at the railing just aft of the second funnel on the port side, staring into the sun's blazing red ball. It hung just above the horizon on a calm cerulean sea that smelled of salt and carried a wind that tingled the skin with its brisk snap. She was dressed in long pants and wore a quilted parka. For a moment, I debated returning to my suite for a heavier jacket, but seeing her there, the breath billowing from her mouth in wispy clouds, and her bemused,

almost melancholy expression, I decided against it. I moved toward her,
and she turned, spotted me, and smiled. "You stood me up, Galahad."

I gave her an exaggerated bow, scraping low with an imaginary
plumed hat. "Your humble servant begs your forgiveness, your
highness."

She came to me, then, her breath hot against my face. "You're
forgiven," she said, and kissed me. Her mouth flowed against mine,
warm and urgent, long nimble fingers raking through my hair. A soft
moan escaped from deep within her chest, and I responded, pulling her
tight against me. She sighed, and I could feel the pounding of her heart.
A boundless moment later she pulled away, breathing heavily, and lay
her head on my shoulder.

"I'm going to have to stand you up more often, if this is what I get,"
I said. She responded by holding me tighter, making me regret my
flippancy. "I'm sorry about dinner, Maddy. I was really looking forward
to it, and to seeing you. I guess I was a lot more tired than I thought."

She lifted her head and studied me, a twinkle of amusement in her
eyes.

"They say the sea air does that, you know. Too much of a good
thing."

She took my hand and we started walking toward the stern, neither
one of us in a hurry to get where we were going.

"Maybe so," I said, "but I think it's also this voyage, too."

"What do you mean?"

"The people I've been interviewing. Their stories are so damned
heartbreaking. And then Mrs. Bates dying so suddenly.... I suppose I'd
hoped the journey would be more...uplifting."

Her hand squeezed mine, though she remained silent.

We reached the end of the Boat Deck a short time later and saw
that a sizeable crowd had already formed. We found an empty spot at
the railing. The entire Poop Deck was crowded with passengers, some
even standing on the docking bridge looking down on the proceedings.
Still others leaned over the railings on A- and B-decks, while the last
few stragglers crowded in behind us.

The only area not jammed with passengers was just forward of the docking bridge near the starboard railing. It was there that Harlan and Captain Pierce stood in whispered conference, while next to them, on a makeshift catafalque consisting of a wide board resting across two benches, lay Mrs. Bates's body wrapped in what appeared to be sailcloth. One end of the board sat on the iron railing; all it would take to send her on her way was for someone to upend the board. Off to the side, with their instruments held at the ready, stood the ship's band, looking cold and uneasy.

Harlan and the captain continued their conference, while everyone waited, the silence broken only by the sound of the wind soughing across the deck. A moment later, the Captain nodded, opened a worn leather-bound book he held clutched in his hands, and began to speak in a clear, resonant voice. "The Lord maketh me to lie down in green pastures. I shall not want...."

The crowd repeated after him, there voices blending into a hushed monotone. Two elderly women, standing a few feet from me, began to cry, and a stoic-looking man in his fifties averted his eyes from mine, his lips trembling. Maddy squeezed my hand harder.

Scant minutes later, the captain finished his bible reading with one of the Psalms, I can't recall which one. I never was the most religious of people, preferring my own private communion with whatever force or being had created the universe. But here, on the deck of this great ship, together with everyone on board looking on, I felt the most profound sense of sadness.

When the captain closed his book, Harlan delivered a eulogy: "Like most of you," he said, his quiet voice carrying across the deck on the wind. "I only knew Eugenia Bates for a brief span. When I first met her during her initial interview, she struck me as a woman who'd lived her life as if every moment were a diamond shining in the sun...."

Harlan continued to speak for another ten minutes, and I was surprised to learn that Mrs. Bates had been a child psychologist, and a mother of four. To my friend's credit, he kept his tendency toward bombast to a minimum, choosing his words with care, compassion and skill. When he was through, he signaled to the band, who raised their instruments and began to play.

When I heard the tune, two emotions fought a tug-of-war inside of me: one prompted me to smile at the obviousness of the choice, while the other urged me to cry, for it *was* the perfect selection.

Nearer My God to Thee.

The band played it with uncommon poignancy, and Maddy began to sob. I held her against me, my arms encircling her from behind. All sorts of images began flooding my mind, then: images from Cameron's monumental film, scenes of sadness from my own life, and the lives of those I'd known. And it all came crashing down on me.

As if she sensed the storm raging within me, Maddy turned and held me to her, whispering soft words of comfort in my ear.

When the song ended some moments later, two crewmen grasped either side of the board on which Mrs. Bates lay in her sailcloth shroud and tilted it up over the railing. For a split second her body remained on the board suspended between our world and the next, and then, all at once, she slid off with a rustle of canvas against wood...and was gone.

Harlan shook Captain Pierce's hand, and then the two of them turned and walked toward the Well Deck stairs, the crowd parting before them. Moments later they descended the stairs and disappeared through a door leading into C-deck. The crowd dispersed immediately, breaking up into small solemn groups, following in their wake. Those on the Boat Deck turned and flowed past us, funneling into the stairway marked, "Second Class Entrance." Ten minutes later, Maddy and I were alone, and during all that time not a word was spoken by anyone.

We stayed for a while longer, watching the wake churned up by the *Titanic's* triple screws, the sun warming our faces while it climbed higher into the sky. Maddy finally broke the silence, speaking in a quiet, determined voice. "I want you to take me to your suite, Trevor."

I stood frozen in place, my hands gripping the railing with white-knuckle intensity. I could hardly believe that the woman who ran from me only two nights before, now wished to give herself to me. I didn't have to be a psychologist to understand that her desire grew out of her close brush with death. By confronting it so directly in what happened to Mrs. Bates, Maddy now wanted affirmation.

I kept my eyes on the ocean, a part of me fearing to look at her and discover her desire to be nothing more than my fantasy. "You don't have to do this, you know," I said, trying to keep the tremor out of my voice.

"I know, but I want to." I turned to her and saw a tiny smile on her face. "And if you weren't such a gentleman," she said, "I'd think you didn't want me."

"Don't you *ever* think that."

I gave her my arm and the two of us strolled back down the length of the Boat Deck.

❖ ❖ ❖

My hand actually trembled when I tried to place my key in the lock, and I hid my embarrassment when Maddy placed hers over mine and guided it in. The old saw about feeling like a schoolboy on his first date definitely applied in this case, but I wasn't about to let it stop me.

Unlocking the door, I swung it open and Maddy swept by me, pulling off her parka and spinning it onto one of the Biedermeier chairs. "My God, this is gorgeous," she said taking in the mahogany paneling and the silk wall covering.

"We'll you're the one who wanted to work her way up to First Class. Congratulations, you made it."

"In more ways than one," she said, a sly grin on her face.

She flew into my arms then, knocking me back onto the bed with a flood of giggles. She was reaching for my belt when Henry came out of the adjoining room carrying my folded laundry. I had to hand it to him, he handled any embarrassment he may have felt with aplomb, and far better than Maddy and I did. We sat up like two guilty teenagers, smoothing our clothes, our eyes darting about the room, as if we expected our mothers to burst in on us next.

Without so much as breaking stride, Henry placed the clothes on the dresser and moved toward the door. "Will you be requiring me anytime before lunch, sir?" he asked, his eyebrows arched.

"Uhh, I think not, Henry."

"Very good, sir."

With that, he left, clicking the door shut behind him.

Maddy looked at me, then burst out laughing, tears streaming from her eyes, her arms clutching her abdomen.

"Oh, God, that hurts," she said, giggling.

By now, I was laughing, too, and our mirth fed off each other as we rolled about on the bed. Gradually our mood shifted, the laughing ceased, and we gazed into each other's eyes across a gulf of uncertainty. This time, it was I who took the lead, my lips meeting hers with a tenderness I'd never felt for anyone before. Kissing her felt so natural, as if we'd been doing it for years, and yet it was fresh and exciting and new.

I went to undress her and she stopped me. "No, I want to undress you, first."

I nodded and watched, my arousal growing while she stripped me piece by piece, always making sure to kiss each portion of me that was exposed. It felt so damned good my jaw ached from gritting my teeth. And what made it even more pleasurable was seeing the delight in her eyes.

I drew her to me, kissed her and said, "Now, it's my turn."

When I reached for her, she drew back, fearful again. "What's wrong, Maddy? Whatever it is, we can get past it."

She sat up, her lip trembling.

"I'm not so sure *you* can, Trevor."

"Seeing as how we're here, what have we got to lose?"

She opened her mouth to speak, then closed it. I could see the wheels of her mind grinding my words round and round, trying to find a way around their logic. She eased herself from the bed, kicked off her shoes, and began unbuttoning her blouse. Just as the last button came undone, she turned and presented me with her back. Next came her pants and her socks. Now, all that were left were her brassiere and panties, black lacy affairs that looked as if they'd come from Victoria's Secret Catalog.

She still stood facing away from me, her slim, athletic body enticing me; and every fiber of my being urged me to go to her, but I refrained.

Whatever precipice she stood at in her mind, she had to make the leap herself, or not at all.

Finally, I saw her exhale a deep breath and turn, a look of awful expectation on her face. Her body was exceptional, well-proportioned and toned. But it only took a fleeting glance to see the root of all her fears: a livid scar nearly half an inch wide ran down the center of her chest between her breasts down to her navel, then curved around her left side, stopping just shy of her back. I could also see marks where, instead of conventional sutures, staples were used to hold the massive incision closed.

She watched every nuance on my face, her eyes wide with dread. I was shocked, certainly, but not in the way one might expect. And I didn't react, at least not as she must have anticipated. Instead of gasping, or looking repulsed, something that would have shattered her, I held out my hand, my eyes locked with hers.

"Come here," I said.

Maddy's eyes flooded with tears and she ran to me, encircling my neck in a tight embrace. "I didn't want to be ugly for you, Trevor," she said, sobbing.

I lifted her chin with my hand and kissed her forehead, her nose, and then her mouth. "You could never be ugly, Maddy, not ever."

And then she gave herself to me....

⊕   ⊕   ⊕

I can't remember how long we made love, time having ceased to have any meaning while in each other's arms. But afterward, with the afternoon sun slanting through the windows, I lay in the crook of her arm, listening to her breathing as she slept. Soon, my own fatigue overcame my desire to remain awake and I drifted off into a restless slumber. This time, however, the vague dreams I'd experienced over the last two nights sharpened into disturbing clarity....

Maddy and I were exploring the bowels of the ship moving through the engine room and the holds. She was giddy with excitement, pulling me toward the bow with an ever-increasing sense of urgency.

For me, the closer we drew, the more I dreaded what we would find there. I tried to pull her back, but she just laughed and dragged me onward, her strength that of someone superhuman.

Finally, after traveling through a labyrinth of cargo holds, far more than really existed, I found myself once again before that locked and guarded watertight door. Only this time, the one guarding it was Cerberus, the three-headed dog of Hades, its six eyes burning coals. And when it saw me, it howled, it's tri-tone voice the screams of uncounted souls in torment.

Behind it the watertight door glowed red, as if superheated, pulsing with an unholy life of its own. Maddy looked at me and smiled, her eyes now surrounded by dark circles, her skin stretched tight on her skull.

"Don't you want to go in, Trevor?" she asked, cackling like a witch. "Don't you want to know what's there?"

"NO!" I screamed, though my voice sounded far away, as if I were at the end of a very long tunnel.

I turned to run, stopping dead in my tracks when I realized that the way we'd come in was now a solid bulkhead of steel. The only way out was through the watertight door. Suddenly, the door dimmed and cracked open. Noxious smoke poured out, smelling of brimstone.

"Go in, Trevor, you know you want to," the Maddy-thing said. Her hair had turned to writhing snakes, and her tongue, oil-black and forked, slithered in and out of her mouth.

And then, I heard a sweet ethereal sound coming from behind me. I turned and saw Julia standing clothed in the raiments of an angel, suffused with a light that was so beautiful it made me ache with desire. "Come back, Trevor," Julia said. "There's nothing for you here."

Desperate, I reached out to Julia, only to have the Maddy-thing pull me back, her grip burning my skin like acid. I screamed in agony. "JULIA! HELP ME! JUUUULIA!"

❖　　❖　　❖

I bolted awake, bathed in a sheen of sweat, another scream dying on my lips.

Maddy held me, rocking me back and forth, her voice a comforting murmur: "It's all right, Trevor, it's all right. It's only a dream! You're awake, and I'm here...."

For a moment, it took all of my will not to push her away, the image of her as Medusa still fresh within my mind. And then the spell broke and I shook my head, laughing at the absurdity of it. "Christ, that was awful. I haven't had nightmares like that since I was a kid, and my mother let me stay up and watch *Dante's Inferno* on television."

"Do you want to tell me about it?"

I shook my head to clear away the last tendrils of fog from my brain; the horrific images and feelings were already fading. Just to be sure, however, I let my eyes roam over the suite. Everything looked the same, the mahogany paneling, brocaded wall covering, the sturdy bedposts, all of it solid, real.

"I don't know if I should," I said finally, wiping the sweat from my eyes. "You were in it, and it wasn't pretty."

"Who's Julia?"

I looked at her then, no longer disturbed by the mythological transformation she'd undergone during my nightmare.

"I talked?"

"Very eloquently, I might add." She laughed. "Come on, it might help to talk it out."

Now, you *sound* like Julia."

"I do, huh?"

"Yes. She's a clinical psychologist. I've known her for about five years."

"Are you in love with her?"

I shot her an incredulous look.

"Don't look so shocked. It's a legitimate question."

"I'm in love with *you*."

Maddy smiled and kissed me. "And I you. But you haven't answered my question."

"Come on, Maddy, how can you even ask me that? After what we've just done."

She laughed again.

"You really are a stick-in-the-mud, aren't you?"

"A what?"

"Oh, you really should see that look on your face, Trevor, it's priceless." She giggled and I became annoyed.

"You mind if I ask you a question? Are you out of your mind?"

"Trevor, I'm as sane as you are, just not as hung up. I happen to believe you can love more than one person at a time. You love your parents, don't you?"

"Yes, but that's different—"

"Not the essential emotion. Tell me more about Julia."

I shook my head, suddenly uncomfortable. "I don't think that's such a great idea."

"For you, or me."

"Both."

She held up her hand, putting a solemn look on her face, though I could see a hint of amusement around the corners of her eyes. "I promise that I will not throw a jealous scene over Julia, now or ever. How about that? Does that ease your mind?"

I shrugged. "Well, I—maybe a little."

"Good, now tell me about her."

"Yes, Ms. Freud. That's what I called her whenever she became too analytical about our lives...."

I spent the next ten minutes filling Maddy in about her rival, and I found that it became easier and easier to reveal things I would never have thought possible about my relationship with Julia. I wound it up by telling her about our last fight over Harlan's *Titanic*, my intention to sail on her, and Julia's fear."

"...So, I guess she had every right to be afraid," I said. "I met you."

"And you're still in love with her."

"How can you say that, Maddy? I don't even know if I was ever in love with her to begin with. And with you there *is* no doubt."

"I say it because I hear it in the way you speak about her, the words you use...and the feelings behind them."

"That's because I'm a writer."

"No. It's because you're a lover."

"All right, all right, I give up, I concede. You're right. I *do* care for her. But not in the same way I care for you. You're not like anyone I've ever known, Maddy."

She smiled, remaining silent.

"What about you?" I said, turning the tables. "Is there someone else?"

"Yes."

Her simple answer held complex repercussions for me, and I was quite unprepared to hear her say that. I was about to respond when a knock sounded on the door.

"Yes, who is it?"

The answer came, slightly muffled by the thick, solid door. "It's Henry, sir. May I come in?"

"Uhh, I don't think it's such a great idea, Henry."

Maddy giggled, burying her face in the pillow.

"I think, sir, that you might change your mind when you see what I've brought."

I threw the covers over us.

"All right, come in."

The door swung open and Henry wheeled in a linen-draped cart, pushing it into the middle of the room. He immediately set about transforming it into a beautifully set table for two, replete with china, silverware, and two burning candles. The food consisted of two covered plates, which he removed from a warming box under the table.

Both Maddy and I watched him work with admiration and a growing appetite. My stomach growled when the tempting odors escaping from under the covers reached my nostrils.

"Henry, you're a real piece of work," I said, smiling.

"So they tell me, sir." He uncorked a bottle of champagne and placed it in an ice bucket. "If you require anything else, please use the buzzer."

He went to the door, and was about to exit, then stopped himself. He turned to us and bowed. "Miss Regehr, it is a pleasure to meet you, even under these somewhat inconvenient circumstances."

"You, too, Henry," she said, stifling another giggle.

Henry smiled and left us, closing the door behind him with a soft click.

"You hungry?" I asked.

"Are you nuts?"

She laughed and bounded from the bed, now completely at ease with me seeing her scar.

We attacked the food, which turned out to be tournedos of beef grilled to perfection and smothered with a bearnaise sauce, accompanied by asparagus and au gratin potatoes.

"Not exactly for the cholesterol impaired," Maddy said, cutting into the beef. She took a bite, her eyes closing in gastronomic ecstasy. "God, this is good."

"It's typical Edwardian fare," I said, pouring us each some of the cold, dry champagne. "Their sole reason for living was to enjoy life to the fullest." I handed her a flute filled with the champagne and she clinked it against mine. "Here's to a wonderful afternoon and the evening to come."

"And to many more just like it," I added.

Maddy's smile dimmed a few degrees when she put the glass to her lips, but I chose to ignore it at the time.

"How many more interviews are you going to conduct?" she asked, pushing the conversation into another realm.

"I haven't really given it a lot of thought, to tell you the truth. I sort of take them as they come."

"Have you decided how you're going to work them into the book?"

I shrugged, taking a bite of the sauce-soaked beef, feeling it melt on my tongue.

"More or less. I'm thinking the best way to approach it is to seed them throughout the manuscript as interludes and counterpoint to the main narrative. I'll leave them as they are, letting them speak for themselves."

"That sounds terrific. Have you written anything yet, and can I read it?"

I told her about my dispatches and the first two chapters I'd written. "I usually don't like people reading my unfinished material, though. It would be like going to the movies and seeing a rough cut without the music and the sound effects. It's not the same."

"I know what you mean. I went through the same thing with my first job, until I realized that my clients had to see things as we went. I'd really like to see what you've done, and I promise not to be judgmental," she said, once again holding up her hand, a twinkle in her eyes.

Rather than argue, I went to my dresser and pulled out my laptop, turning it on as I handed it to her. Standing behind her, I called up my word processor and pulled up the two files. "When you finish, just close out the program," I said, moving back to my seat. I watched her eyes scanning the screen for a moment, then turned my attention back to the meal, though my stomach now tightened with apprehension.

What I'd said to her about people reading unfinished material was only half-true. Unfinished material was exactly that—unfinished, and I often changed many things before I considered a piece "finished." The other reason I didn't do it was because I couldn't stand *watching* someone read my writing. It was sheer agony. And this time was worse than most, for I truly cared what Maddy thought of it, more so than the potential millions who would eventually read it.

I was just finishing the last of my potatoes when she snapped off the power to the computer, closed its lid and laid it gently on the table. Her expression was unreadable, and that somehow made it worse than if she wore a visible frown. "What did you think?" I asked, trying to appear nonchalant while I examined the dessert. It was a pastry confection I could not readily identify, but which under normal circumstances would have tempted me.

"You want the truth, or the sugar-coated version?"

I collapsed back in to the chair, exhaling a defeated sigh. I then met her gaze head on. "The truth, and nothing less."

She continued to stare at me with that same flat expression to the point where I was ready to scream, then cracked a wide grin. "It's one of the best things I've ever read."

"Really?" I said, relieved and excited all at once.

"I kept wanting it to go on. When I reached the last page, and it wouldn't scroll any further, I actually got angry with you."

Well, that explained her initial reaction.

"I'm so glad you feel that way, you've really made my day."

She shot me a mock-indignant look. "Oh, and the last couple of hours was just chopped liver, I suppose?"

I grinned. "Decidedly not. But writers work so damned hard to keep their readers entertained and engrossed in their make-believe worlds, that we're starved for any kind of praise. Don't get me wrong, having a best seller and the money that comes from it is beyond great, but it's not the same as one reader telling you you've made a difference in their lives."

Maddy refilled our champagne glasses, then raised hers. "To your success."

We drank and then fell silent, both of us unsure what to say next. Maddy finally broke the stalemate. "So...am I going to be in it?" she asked in a quiet voice, staring down at her hands.

"If you'll let me interview you."

She shook her head, suddenly angry.

"I can't, I told you that!"

"Why, Maddy? It's not as if we're strangers anymore."

If I expected her to be reasonable at this point, I was in for a rude awakening. She stood up and began to dress, yanking on her clothes with swift angry moves.

I rose from my chair, went to her, and tried to take her in my arms. She shrugged me off and continued putting on her clothes.

"All right, I'm sorry," I said, backing off. "Just forget I mentioned it, okay?"

She looked at me, her eyes clouded with tears. "I'm sorry, too, Trevor, but you just wouldn't understand how it is."

I threw up my hands. "Why don't you try me? If you trust me enough with your heart, you ought to be able to talk about it. It can't be that bad."

"It's bad," she said, pulling on her blouse.

"Okay, maybe you're right. Maybe I can't ever understand how it is, but being raped is not the end of the world, you know. People get past it."

She stopped moving and stared at me, her jacket half on, a look of astonishment on her face, and then, incredibly, she laughed. It was a laugh that sounded more like a sob. "Is *that* what you think? That I was *raped?*"

"How else do I explain what happened on the promenade the other night. When I started to touch your breast, you flipped out."

Maddy shook her head, another fat tear rolling down her face. "Oh, Trevor, you really don't understand anything, do you? I'll see you later, okay?"

And without waiting for my answer, she stormed out of the suite, leaving me in utter bewilderment.

Henry entered a couple of minutes later and began clearing away the dishes, leading me to wonder if he'd been hovering outside and how much he'd heard. If he *had* heard anything, he pretended otherwise.

And I didn't enlighten him. I wasn't in the mood for his advice at the moment, anyway.

I had Henry draw me a bath and I spent the next twenty minutes soaking, trying to sort out what had just happened. Nothing I came up with made any sense, so I decided to try and salvage what I could of the day and do some work. It was time to find another interviewee.

After toweling off, I dressed in simple casual clothes: a pair of khaki trousers and a polo shirt and a sweater, my normal working attire. I then grabbed my DVD recorder, made my way up to the First Class Lounge and scoped out the inhabitants. I spied a young man seated in a comfortable chair reading a book. When I drew closer, I smiled. The book was one of mine, and it gave me the perfect entre.

"Excuse me, but would you mind if I asked you some questions. The young man looked up from his book, a preoccupied look on his face and a refusal on his lips. Then he focused on my face, recognition blooming in his widening eyes.

"I'm sorry, I didn't recognize you, at first," he said, standing up. "I really enjoy your work."

He extended his hand, and I shook it, feeling his cool flesh against mine.

"Thank you, I appreciate that." I pointed to the book. "What part are you up to?"

"The part where Conrad is being pressured by the Don to become his daughter's bodyguard."

I nodded, smiling. "There's a good part coming up."

"Oh, don't tell me, don't tell me," he said, smiling.

"I wouldn't dream of it, Mister...."

"Kevin, Kevin Subleski." He stuck out his hand again, then remembering that we'd already shaken hands, withdrew it, placing it awkwardly into his pocket. The other one hung onto the book, a finger stuck into the pages to hold his place.

"Would you like me to sign that for you?"

"Would you?"

"My pleasure."

He handed me the volume and, being careful not to lose his place, I took out my pen and wrote him a little note, then signed my name in a sweeping style I developed just for giving autographs.

One thing I could never abide was waiting to get someone's autograph, only to find that they'd signed it in an illegible scrawl. I always made it a point of honor that every signature I penned was a work of art. "There you go," I said, handing it to him.

"Gee, thanks," he said. "You said you wanted to ask me some questions?"

"Yes. Why don't we sit down, if that's okay?"

"Oh, sure," he said, plopping back down into his reading chair. I pulled one up catercorner and placed my DVD recorder onto the small coffee table between us. He watched me insert a disk, and I took the time to examine him out of the corner of my eye. He was exceedingly tall, and gangly, looking like a young Abe Lincoln, whom he resembled in other superficial ways. His hair was a reddish brown and hung down about his angular face in a boyish cut that looked as if it defied styling of any kind. And though he appeared to be what many would call provincial, his hazel eyes were bright and intelligent.

"You need character quirks for a new book? That why you want to talk to me?"

"Something like that," I said, reaching for the start button.

The disk began to spin and the record light snapped on.

13

Interview with Kevin Subleski
Location: First Class Lounge

"What one of the new recorders?" Kevin asked, his fascination with my device clearly evident.

"Takes the mini-DVDs," I replied. "Each disk lasts about an hour."

The young man nodded, an easy grin playing across his face.

"Well, I hope I'll give you your money's worth. What did you want to know?"

I told him.

"All right, then. Like I said, my name is Kevin Subleski, I'm thirty years old and I've spent the better part of my life trying to find out what I wanted to be when I grew up. Sounds pretty sixties, huh?

"I was raised in one of those one-horse burgs outside Dallas, the kind of small town everybody wishes they lived in. Well, let me tell you, it's no different than living in a big city. The only difference is that you know the person who's screwing you. Actually, my childhood was pretty good, for the most part. My parents were dyed-in-the-wool Baptists. Didn't drink, smoke, play cards, or dance. Real straitlaced. I guess that's why when I hit the teenage years, I got kind of wild, you know?"

I smiled. "I can guess."

"Well, let me save you the effort. I took to alcohol like I was born to it. You know, I read that addiction is genetic, and I've often wondered whether my Mom or Dad were alcoholics and were suppressing it, 'cause of their religion, sort of a latent thing. Anyway, me and my buddies began drinkin' and carryin' on something awful. Got arrested a few times. I tell you my parents were fit to be tied. But the funny thing was, as God-fearing as they were, they were afraid to hit me or do anything to discipline me, for fear I'd hate 'em or something."

"But it all changed, didn't it?"

Kevin nodded, "Yes, sir, it did. My mom got cancer when I turned eighteen, raced through her like water running downhill. She was dead inside of two months. After that, my father kind of fell apart. He spent the next year and a half moping around until he had a heart attack one day sitting on the john. I was an orphan at twenty."

"How did you feel about that?"

Kevin stared at his big hands, the fingernails bitten to the quick. "You want the truth? Yes, I suppose that's the point of all this, isn't it? Truth was, I was relieved. I had nothing left to hold me in that dusty little town.

"First thing I did was take the money my parents left me and hit the road. I made it my goal to hitch from Maine to Alaska in a year. Took me two and a half, and damned near killed me. I ended up in a hospital in Nome with frostbite on both feet, lost half my toes. I spent my twenty-third birthday in the hospital. One good thing, though.... When I told the night nurse, she gave me the best present a kid could have. Snuck back in after my roommate had fallen asleep and screwed my brains out. She was a pretty little thing, though not much in the attic, if you know what I mean. Anyway, after I healed, I headed down the Pacific Coast, working my way with odd jobs. Some of them actually paid pretty well, as I recall. It was another year 'fore I reached Los Angeles."

"You stayed there for a while?"

Kevin nodded, that easy grin coming back.

"I hung around some of the studios and managed to luck into extra work. Maybe you've seen me? I was in a couple of sitcoms, one where I was featured every week. Never had any lines though, director said my accent was too thick. Hell, I should have tried out for a Western series, or something.

"I see you're still wondering how I came to be on this boat, aren't you?"

"It did cross my mind," I said, smiling.

"Well, don't you worry, I'm getting to it. Thing is, I was really enjoying the Hollywood lifestyle, such as I was able to partake. When I wasn't working as an extra, I parked cars for a valet service that did all the big parties in Beverly Hills and Hollywood. And let me tell you, I met lots of film folks. Most of the guys would joke with you when you handed them their keys, and if you laughed hard enough, they'd lay a nice tip on you. I learned to laugh real hard.

"The ladies were a different story, the ones who had studio jobs. See, I'm not a chauvinist, not like you'd think a Texan would be. I think a woman should be able to do anything she puts her mind to—and get the same pay for it. No, my problem is that some of them get this attitude, like they know better than anyone what's the right decision to make. Anyway, this lady executive at a party I was working had me get her car and I make this offhand remark about this script I saw sitting on her passenger seat. Told her I thought it was a lousy title."

"Don't tell me, she got you fired."

"Yep. The next day my boss calls me and tells me to come and pick up my check. When I asked him what had happened, he didn't want to tell me at first, but we'd been friendly before, and I broke him down. He told me the bitch—excuse my language—had complained that I'd gone through her things. Now, I never would do that. The title was right there on the spine of the script in black magic marker. You couldn't miss it, especially 'cause it was so lame."

"So, what did you do?"

"A part of me wanted to confront her and tell her what for. But the other part, the one that reins in all my boyish fantasies about getting even, held me back. I decided it wasn't worth the trouble. So I went on home.

"Wouldn't you know it, she was waiting outside my little hole-in-the-wall in her big Mercedes. Seeing her there, I got angry all over again, thought she'd come to rub it in. Turns out, she'd got to feeling bad about what she'd done, told me I was right, that it *was* a lame title, and did I have a better one?"

"Did you?"

Kevin laughed.

"She thought so. Hired me on the spot. From there it was easy street. And it turns out Robin, that's her name by the way, had the hots for me. It wasn't too long before we were keeping company in and out of the office. We went to all the A-list parties and I met everyone who was anyone, got real friendly with a couple of famous actors, and we all hung out everywhere.

"Now, I promised to get around to your question, didn't I? Well, about a year after Robin and I became an item, we were invited to a party over at some bigwig's house up in the hills, had this house perched up on stilts with a view you'd kill for. Turns out he was showing the director's cut of *Titanic* as part of the fun. I think maybe Cameron was there, too, but I didn't see him. Now, you're going to laugh. Up until that time, I'd never seen the film. Oh, I'd heard all about it, I mean, who hasn't? It's only the biggest thing of all time, right?

"Anyway, when Robin heard I hadn't ever seen it, she dragged me into that screening room and plopped me down. And all she said was, 'I envy you,' just like that."

"And...."

"Well, three and a half hours later, I knew what she meant. Seeing that movie for the first time was like a lot of firsts, some of which I need not mention. Aside from being put through the emotional wringer, something no movie had ever done to me, it left something with me, a little kernel of itself. I can't really describe it. Call it haunting, maybe. Yeah, I'd have to say it haunted me. I knew I had to see it again, if nothing else to see if it just wasn't a fluke, a one-time thing. Turns out, Robin, had the DVD version at home, the one that's got all the 'making of' stuff on it.

"I watched it for the second time a week later, and let me tell you it walloped me even harder. I started crying during the opening credits.

That music, the piece with that Norwegian woman singing? Man, it just cuts right through your soul, you know?"

I knew. I knew exactly. "So how did you hear about Harlan's *Titanic*?"

"I suppose it was when the news broke back in February. I was in my doctor's waiting room and CNN was on. As soon as the story started running, I was called into my appointment. Well, I made them wait while I watched it. From the moment I heard about it, I knew I wanted to be on it's first voyage, that it would be something special.

"Funny thing, it's turned out to be more special than I'd ever imagined. You see, the reason I was at my doctor that day was because I'd started feeling poorly, had been for two months. I'd wake up lightheaded and weak, and the feeling would hang with me the whole day. Still, I was a stubborn cuss when it comes to going to the doctor; and the only reason I went was because Robin threatened to leave me if I didn't. So, I went." Kevin paused, his mouth tightening. "I got to give those medical boys credit where it's due. They ran every kind of test imaginable. You name it, they poked and prodded me with it. The long and the short of it was I had what they called a 'pernicious' form of leukemia; my only hope of surviving it was a bone marrow transplant.

"Robin was beside herself, but she really kept it together for me, paid all my bills and started trying to locate a donor. See, my problem is that I have a real rare type: AB negative. I hear it's something like one percent of the population have that. When the weeks and months went by and there was still no donor that matched, I tried one last thing. You remember hearing about that DNA project?"

"You mean the one where they clone bone marrow material from a dead relative?"

"That's the one. My one hope at that point was exhuming my parents and hoping they weren't too far gone. You see, them being Baptists, they didn't believe in embalming. For them the right and holy thing was getting back to the dust as fast as nature would allow. With them being dead for almost a decade, I didn't know if I had a shot in Hell. I know it's kind of creepy, and if I wasn't dying I sure as hell would think so, too. But my options were used up.

"I know I'm going on, but you did want to hear this, didn't you? Anyway, to cut to the chase, both my parents were what the morticians call skeletalized, and the DNA was too far gone to re-map. It was the day that I found this out that I decided I wanted this one last thing in my life: to sail on this ship. You been finding others saying this?"

"Yes, it seems Harlan has allowed a good many ill people on this voyage."

"And I'll bet you didn't know that he paid for my ticket out of his own pocket. Not that Robin couldn't afford it, but he wouldn't take it, ripped up her check and sent it back with the ticket."

"My friend has a big heart."

"You're damn right he does. When I e-mailed him that I wanted to sail on the new *Titanic*, he set up a video interview for the next day. The rest, well, here I am." He sat back in his chair, looking tired and satisfied. "Is that what you wanted, Mr. Hughes? Did I do okay?"

"You did just fine. I have only a couple of more questions. Is that okay?"

"Sure, no problem. Shoot."

"Why isn't Robin with you?"

"I'd rather not talk about that."

"You and she break up?"

"You might say that."

"Okay, last question.... Has the voyage been worth it?"

Kevin remained silent for a minute, then looked me directly in the eyes, his expression sober. "Every damn minute."

14

Dinner that evening proved anticlimactic. Besides myself, the only other occupants at the table were Hoyt Asbury, as churlish as ever, and Gavin Reynolds, who managed to spend the entire meal in self-absorbed silence. But it was the three empty chairs that disturbed me the most: Mrs. Bates's, Harlan's...and Maddy's.

From what little I could pry out of our steward, Harlan had decided to take his meal in his suite. He'd looked tired the last time I'd seen him, and was no doubt taking it easy. That didn't bother me, other than I missed his wit and style. With Maddy, it was a different story. I'd hoped to see her and take the opportunity to apologize for what had happened in my suite. It seemed that with her I couldn't help putting my foot in it, in one fashion or another. And what did that spell for us down the road?

I'd begun to realize the voyage would be over in a few days and I had a book to write, which meant a lot of hard work and solitude, hardly the stuff on which to build a long-term relationship.

And then there was the fact that we both lived in different cities. Even though she'd retired from interior design, was it reasonable to expect that she would move to Boston, give up her old life for mine?

And what about me?

Would I move to New York for her, a city that I loved to visit but loathed living in? Did each of us love the other enough to make that sacrifice? And others?

I knew the answer for me was an unequivocal, yes. But what did Maddy *really* feel for me? Did she love me the same? More? Less?

The answers eluded me. Too many questions assaulted me while I sat there in my evening clothes trying to eat the rich food that was becoming ever more cloying by the mouthful. I longed for a sloppy burger, or a pizza from Santarpios, that much-loved landmark in East Boston. Anything but fancy French food with a heavy, highly-caloric sauce poured over it.

With my stomach turning somersaults, and a dull ache throbbing behind the eyes, I made my excuses and left the dining saloon for the solitude of the Boat Deck, where I wandered for over an hour in the evening chill in the hopes I would run into Maddy. I was out of luck there, too. Like Harlan, she'd apparently decided to stay in.

Annoyed and concerned, I took one of the lifts down to E-deck and stood in front of her door an entire minute before knocking. As with the last time in steerage, she did not answer. Either she was not in, or she was refusing to acknowledge me, something that both angered and worried me. After five minutes, I gave up and returned to my suite and put in a solid two hours of writing. I was just finishing the third chapter when I heard a soft knocking. My heart soared, thinking it was Maddy, and my face must have made a silly picture when I threw open the door and found Sammy Richards standing in the hall, his fist poised for another knock.

"Sorry to bother you, Mr. Hughes," he said, "but you have a Marconigram."

I hid my disappointment and took the proffered paper from him.

"Is everything all right, Mr. Hughes? You look a little worried."

I smiled and nodded. "Everything's fine, Sammy. Just trying to get the words right."

He glanced over my shoulder and saw my laptop sitting on the small writing table, its screen glowing in the darkness. "Oh, I get you," he said, looking embarrassed "Sorry to bother you. Have a good night."

He nodded, then retraced his steps toward the Wireless Room. I closed the door, went back and sat down in front of my computer, then unfolded the Marconigram.

I shook my head, a weary smile curling my lips. The message was from Marty. It said: *You never call me anymore. Got some interesting dope. Give me a ring.*

I hadn't wanted any contact with the outside world, preferring to immerse myself in the allure of Harlan's *Titanic* for the duration. Now, with Marty's not-so-subtle appeal, I decided to end my self-imposed "radio silence."

Closing out my word processor, I then opened up the cellular software, using the number keys to dial Marty's private number. A minute later, I was staring into his bleary-eyed face.

"Hi, Marty, I got your message."

"About time, kid. You wouldn't believe the gyrations I've gone through to send one of those stupid Macaronigrams."

"Marconi."

Marty frowned. "What?"

"It's a *Marconi*gram."

"Whatever," he said, shrugging.

"So, what's up?"

"How's your friend, Harlan?"

"What do you mean?"

"I mean, how is he? Is he feeling all right?"

"Marty, what's this all about? Since when do you care about anything other than your business."

"'Cause it *is* my business. Just answer the question."

"I don't know, all right, I guess."

"You don't know?"

"No, Marty, I don't. Can we cut to it, it's late and I've got more work to do."

The agent perked up at the mention of work.

"Oh, yeah? You cookin' up something good?"

"Marty, why are you asking about Harlan?"

"It seems your buddy's been winding up his affairs."

I shook my head. "What are you talking about?"

"I'm talking about dotting the I's and crossing the T's, that sort of thing."

Marty was never the type to beat around the bush, so seeing him do it now, bothered the hell out of me.

"Marty, you're getting obscure on me."

"It's probably nothing. But I got the skinny from a source of mine that told me he's put all his affairs in order prior to the voyage, that's all. Probably nothing."

"It's definitely nothing. I've known Harlan a long time. He's a meticulous planner. He's just preparing for every contingency, like he does with everything. Hell, it's the same kind of thinking that motivates some people to buy flight insurance every time they get on a plane. You worried, Marty?"

The agent shook his head, his jowls quivering like Jell-O. "I always worry about my clients. Besides, I'm superstitious."

He was right about that. Marty had the biggest collection of rabbit's feet I've ever seen.

"I know, that's why I'm here and you're not. So, what else is going on."

"Mannheim Books is getting hotter to trot by the minute, kid. When do you think you'll have a draft?"

"Probably a few days after I get back. This deadline's going to kill me."

"I know, I don't envy you, but I know I can depend on you."

"That you can."

"All right, kid, keep me posted."

I rung off and reopened my word processor, managing to write another two thousand words before Henry let himself into the suite to turn down my bed at eleven o'clock.

"Have you had a good evening, sir?" he asked, folding down the coverlet.

"Depends on what you mean."

He eyed me with an expression of concern, not once hesitating in duties. "Perhaps the lady wishes a little space, as the young so handily put it."

I snapped off the computer and clicked it shut, accompanying it with a sigh of weariness. "Sure, why not. She falls in love one day and wants space the next. Makes as much sense as anything else on this voyage. My best friend builds his dream and spends most of it in his cabin. Does that make sense to you, Henry?"

The older man finished smoothing out the sheets and turned to me. "May I be frank, sir?"

I looked up at him then, thinking he was being wry, finding him meeting my gaze with a sober expression without even a hint of his dry humor.

"I wish you would," I said finally.

"There are things about this voyage to which you are not privy. And I think it would be best if you concentrated on your present task. You will be much happier for it."

If his words were intended to comfort me, they had the opposite effect. "Wait a minute. What *things* are you talking about?"

Henry shook his head. "I'm sorry, sir, but while I am assigned to you, I also work for Mr. Astor—"

I stood up and crossed the room, my anger growing. "I don't give a damn who you work for, you don't presume to give me advice by dangling vague information in front of me like that and not elaborate."

I saw Henry stiffen, all of our easy rapport now gone. "I'm sorry, I should not have said anything. Please use the bell if you require anything else."

And with that he left me to the rising tide of doubts swirling about in my mind. I debated going after him, but the longer I hesitated, the less likely I would be able to find him. I had no idea where he slept, and I knew in my heart of hearts that he was too loyal to Harlan to betray a confidence. Besides, I was probably making more of it than it was, something I was very adept at doing.

Fatigue overcame me then, and I trudged into the bathroom to complete my evening ablutions. By the time I climbed into bed some twenty minutes later, I was too tired to worry about anything. I fell asleep within five minutes.

The dream came again, the Dantean imagery even more vivid and horrific than before. The essential difference between this one and the last was that the roles Julia and Maddy played were reversed. Now,

Maddy was the angel trying to lead me back from Hell, and Julia was Medusa with her writhing serpentine locks.

This time, I woke up screaming, the sweat soaking my bedclothes. I sat up and snapped on the light, my heart hammering against my ribs, and tried to focus my mind on the details of the dream. One thing *did* emerge from the murk of my subconscious: *the watertight door.* The whole of my nightmare centered around that one part of the ship supposedly off-limits to the passengers and guarded by the burly crewman. Whatever it was that lay behind that door was preying on my subconscious, forcing my sleeping mind to confront it. Why it was doing so in such a stylized manner was anyone's guess, and I supposed that even Julia would be hard-pressed to interpret it with any certainty. And yet, I knew one thing absolutely: *I had to find out what was behind that door.*

I threw aside the blankets and sheets, changed into the clothes I'd worn the day before, and left the suite a few minutes later. It was past three in the morning and the ship now ran on a skeleton crew. As I made my way down the hall toward the Grand Staircase, I suddenly realized that the vibration of the ship felt different, somehow. More rapid. And then it hit me....

We were going faster.

Just as in the original voyage, when Captain Smith had ordered the ship's speed increased to twenty-two knots so, it seemed, had we.

The trip to the holds beneath the forecastle took far less time than it had the first day of the voyage when the vastness of the *Titanic* had so overwhelmed me. When I drew closer to the Number One watertight door, my breathing accelerated and my pulse pounded in my ears. The vibration of the ship's engines were the least up here toward the bow but, if one listened carefully, one could hear the sounds of the water rushing alongside. As it was, it was deathly quiet. Peeking around the corner, I was startled to discover the door unguarded. Perhaps at this late hour Harlan had not felt the need to be so vigilant, or maybe he'd grown less concerned about compromising whatever lay behind it, now trusting that his passengers were less likely to venture below, the novelty having worn thin.

Whatever the reason, it appeared Providence had given me the chance to satisfy my curiosity. I moved out from behind my hiding place and over to the watertight door itself. A massive thing, the door could be operated remotely from the bridge, or manually from where I stood via a button set into a panel. One button was green the other red. Exhaling the last of my fear, I reached up and pushed the green button, startled as the sound of a motor began whining, overlaid by the sound of clanking gears. The fear came rushing back. Intent as I was on getting the door open, I had not checked out the immediate surroundings to make sure no one lurked about. I had assumed that I was safe. A potentially fatal error. And though it appeared I was safe, for the moment, the fear remained, for I realized with a rush of dread that the sounds had also been in my dreams.

The door cranked upward at a snail's pace, at least it seemed that way to me. Finally, when the opening was wide enough to admit a man, I stooped and crawled through, barking my shins on the bulkhead.

I stood just inside the door, waiting while my eyes adjusted to the gloom. The entire hold was perhaps a thousand square feet, the white-painted steel walls narrowing steeply toward the bow, which lay hidden behind more of Harlan's bogus cargo. Crates upon crates lay stacked to the ceiling, battened down with coarse hemp netting. The air inside was hot and smelled musty. There was no light switch that I could find, nor was there a way to close the door from the inside, leaving me vulnerable should anyone return.

A sweat broke out on my skin and I felt it trickling down my spine. It was time to move, yet something prevented my legs from obeying my brain. Fear seemed an inadequate word to describe the feeling that enveloped me. I staggered forward, first one step, then another. I kept expecting flames to sprout from the walls and the Medusa to appear, cackling wildly. My rational mind knew it was silly, yet the remnant of the reptilian brain that all of us share from our earliest ancestors kept warning me.

Something is wrong, it said.

My anxiety rising, I forced myself onward into the room, squeezing by the crates. I had no idea what I was looking for. It might have been anything. And if it resided inside one of the sealed crates I was already defeated, for I had no way of breaking into them, no crowbar. Nor did I have the time. There had to be over fifty crates in all.

In spite of this, I took the time to examine as many as I could see without undoing the hemp netting holding them in place. As far as I could tell, there was nothing at all sinister about them. It was now approaching four in the morning, and I was tired, frustrated, and angry. Why would Harlan have someone guard the hold, if there was nothing *worth* guarding? Logic dictated, therefore, that there *must* be something there. I was about to leave, when something caught my eye, something red and luminous. It took me a moment to focus. It was against the far wall, nestled against the hull plating where it met the bulkhead.

My anger forgotten for the moment, I crossed the room, bending down for a closer look. It appeared to be a plain black box made from steel or aluminum and painted with a black wrinkle finish, and was attached to the plating by some kind of super-hard aircraft epoxy. Springing from it were dozens of micro-fine insulated wires, so skillfully placed along the seams of the hull plating that I would never have noticed them, except that each one terminated into the head of a rivet.

What had initially attracted my eye, however, was a red LED readout, divided into hours, minutes, and seconds. The seconds were even now flashing by in rapid descending order: *41:39:45... 41:39:44...41:39:43....*

Math never being my strong suit in school, it took me several moments of mental fumbling before I determined that the timer would reach zero at approximately 11:40 p.m. on April 14th, two days hence.

A cold shiver swept through me when I realized the significance of that date and time: *the moment the original* Titanic *struck the iceberg.*

"My God, Harlan, what are you doing?" I said, breaking the silence.

"Hey, what the hell are you doing down here?"

I swung around as the burly crewman's shadow fell upon me. The man's face was flushed with blood, angry.

Reacting without thought, I threw myself at him, knocking him back against a heavy crate. He made an "Oooof" sound and bent over double.

I ran.

Diving through the open watertight door, I rolled to my feet and slammed my fist down on the red "down" button, now relieved beyond measure to hear that metallic clanking.

"YOU!"

I whirled and spotted another crewman with sandy hair and a snarl on his lips, barreling toward me. Panicking, I took off, heading for the safety of one of the other holds. A part of me, the mindless primitive, knew that if I could get back to my suite, I would be safe. The rational part knew otherwise: *that all roads led back to Harlan, and there was no place safe—except off the boat.*

My pace slowed when I reached the next hold. Like the last one, it was filled with more *ersatz* cargo, as well as Harlan's painstaking re-creation of William Carter's 1912 maroon Renault. I stared at it, no longer seeing it as a nostalgic reminder of a tender, romantic moment from Cameron's film. Now, it became a symbol of all the waste, of all the money he'd spent on the greatest of living monuments, and now made ready to destroy. The question was: why?

The two crewman caught up with me at that moment, each of them taking one arm. The big one shook me angrily. "You've got a lot of explainin' to do, mate," he said, in a thick Cockney dialect.

The other one, shorter and far slighter than his muscular companion stared at me with wild eyes. "What'll we do with him, Charley?"

"We'll take him to the Squire, we will." He turned to me, gripping my arm harder. It felt as if it was caught in a vise. "And no funny business, or we'll bloody well toss you over the bleedin' side."

I shook my arms free, and stared him down. "Yes, you do that. And see what Mr. Astor has to say about it."

Charley's eyes narrowed in anger, but I saw the wheels turning laboriously in his brain. It didn't take him long to realize his threat was an empty one. He grabbed me again and the blonde one followed suit. "Come on, you," Charley said, pulling me toward the door. My last glimpse of the Renault and the hull plating beyond it revealed more of the micro-fine wiring, more explosive rivets.

Ten minutes later, after climbing interminable stairs—the lifts were shut down for the night—we stood in front of Harlan's suite, the steward guarding it giving us the once over. Charley nodded. "There's a good lad. Open up."

The steward looked nervous. "He said he didn't want to be disturbed."

"We found this bloke in the Number One hold. I think he'll want to know. Now open the bloody door!"

The door swung open behind the steward and Harlan stood there, glaring, wrapped in his silk dressing gown. I tried to hide my shock at his appearance. The skin on his face had taken on a crepey appearance, the color a sickening jaundiced hue. The eyes, surrounded by deep circles the color of putty, burned in their sockets with righteous anger.

"What the hell is going on out here?" he shouted, spittle flying from his cracked, dry lips.

Charley's bravado dimmed somewhat, but he thrust me forward with little effort. I felt like a rag doll in his hands. "We found this bloke in Number One."

Harlan turned and fixed his gaze upon me, his expression softening. "I guess I should have expected this from you, kiddo," he said, sadly.

I didn't answer him, my anger and confusion overwhelming me at that moment.

He nodded to the two crewmen. "Bring him in, Charley. And you," he said to the blonde crewman, "go back to your post. And don't leave it again."

The crewman blanched. "Yes, sir, Mr. Astor."

He scuttled off and Charley shoved me into the suite. I stumbled against one of the Louis Quinze chairs, nearly toppling it. I shot the burly crewman a hateful glare and stood up.

"That'll be enough, Charley," Harlan said, shutting the door and advancing into the suite. Gone was the bounce in his step. He crossed the floor in slow motion, as if his joints were in excruciating pain. How,

I wondered, could a man who looked so healthy a few days before have declined so alarmingly? Unless his appearance was merely that. Artifice covering something grave, something dark and all-consuming.

"Why, Harlan?" I said, finally finding my voice.

"I think you know, Trev."

He eased himself into one of the chairs, his expression twisting into a grimace.

"Pretend I don't. Spell it out for me."

"Why? Do you think I owe you an explanation?"

I advanced on him, my eyes blazing.

"Hell, yes! You're the one who wanted me on this godforsaken tub. Yes, you owe me!"

Charley, who'd taken up a station in front of the door, moved toward me menacingly. Harlan waved him back with a weak flip of his hand. The big man appeared edgy, and I was sincerely grateful that he was not armed with anything more than his bare hands, though those ham-sized appendages looked as if they could well be deadly if required.

"I'm dying, kiddo," Harlan said, staring at the floor. "Liver cancer. At least that's where it started. Can you believe it? And it seems like only yesterday that we were kids having keg parties at the frat house."

Had he told me this at any other time, I would have been rocked to the core, stunned beyond belief. Now, in light of what I'd seen down in the Number One hold, it barely mattered, and came as no surprise. The signs had been there all along from that time back in the Harvard Club. I'd simply chosen to ignore the obvious.

"What about the timer?"

He looked up at me then, his eyes welling with tears. "It's an explosive device, as you surmised, old friend. Each wire is connected to an explosive rivet. When they detonate, the hull will open to the sea and—"

"The *Titanic* will founder, breaking in half and sinking in two and half hours."

Harlan nodded, his eyes closed.

For a brief instant I was rendered mute by the enormity of his ego.

And then I exploded, grabbing him by the collar of his dressing gown and shaking him. "How can you do this! Just because you and a few others on this ship are dying, you're going to kill them all?"

Charley pulled me off of him with terrifying ease, once again making me feel as if I were a plaything. Harlan collapsed back into his chair, his breathing ragged. He pulled a pillbox from out of his dressing gown, opened it and popped a tiny white pill into his mouth. He then grabbed for a water glass on the table next to his chair, both hands shaking as he brought it to his lips and took a swallow. Sighing, he replaced the glass on the table and regarded me with hooded eyes.

"I could have Charley break you in half for that."

"Go ahead."

A thin smile twisted his lips. "You always were the melodramatic type, kiddo. That's why I wanted you along, to tell our story the way it should be told—from the heart."

"And what story is that? Harlan's Grand Guignol? Come one, come all?"

"I wanted death with dignity, goddamn it! Not rotting away in some fucking hospital room smelling my own piss and shit!"

"What about all those lofty words about this ship being a symbol for a 'rebirth of spirit?' Is that all it was? Just so much bullshit?"

Harlan remained silent, his expression stony.

"All right. So, you want to go down with your ship. That's just grand. What about the others? What about what *they* want?"

"You make it sound so selfish," Harlan said, the hurt evident in his voice. He turned to the burly crewman. "Why don't you tell my friend what you want, Charley."

The big man turned toward me, his face losing all its menace.

"You wouldn't know it to look at me, but I've been fighting the big 'C' for years. Last checkup the doc said I had maybe five months. I had nothin' left to me name. No family, no money, *nothin'*. The Guv'nor, here, gave me the chance to go out with me dignity in a way that would mean something." Tears welled in the big man's eyes, and he used the back of a hand to wipe them away. "This old tub was something I'd loved since I was a kid. Ever since I seen that movie...."

"You see, Trev?" Harlan said, interrupting when it became clear that Charley couldn't go on. "Except for the dozen who changed their minds and left on Mayor Donahue's launch, it's the same for all of them, or didn't you get that sense when you interviewed them?"

He was right.

Though none of the people I'd interviewed had voiced it, I could tell they were serene—all their troubles behind them. For them, the *Titanic* was a symbol not only for an end, but also for a beginning.

Then again, I couldn't help wondering about the shy dentist from Joliet I'd interviewed early on the second day. He'd seemed torn and conflicted, and had stuttered throughout the entire interview. I hadn't seen him since Cobh. Could he have been among those who'd left the ship? If so, I wished him well. I nodded my head, feeling ineffably sad, yet accepting my friend's wishes. "When am I leaving the ship?"

"You have until tomorrow at sundown," he said.

"Don't you want me to be here for the—"

"No...." he said, shaking his head. "I don't want to risk anything happening to you if things go wrong. I've prepared one of the lifeboats for you, number nine, I think. You'll have food and water for five days. And there's a satellite phone, as well. But I want your word you won't use it until dawn on the fifteenth. Do I have it?"

"Yes."

"I'm sorry I couldn't tell you about this at the beginning. I didn't want you talking me out of it."

"It's too bad you couldn't trust me, Harlan. Now, if you'll excuse me, I'm going to tell Maddy, that is if I can find her."

Harlan hesitated, then shook his head. "She won't be going with you, Trev...."

"Don't you think that's her decision?"

"Yes, and she's already made it."

I felt as if the world were tilting beneath my feet, a part of me denying what the rest of me knew.

"What are you talking about?"

"My God, she didn't tell you," he said, his eyes widening. "She's dying, too, Trev. Just like the rest of us—just like *everyone* aboard this ship. Except you. You're the only one with a life expectancy over six months."

"GODDAMN YOU!" I snatched up a bottle of Chivas sitting on a nearby table and hurled it at the wall. He barely reacted when it sailed past him, missing by inches, and shattered on the mahogany paneling.

I had no chance to do anything else.

Charley launched himself at me with a wordless cry, and we landed on one of the Louis Quinze chairs, which splintered under our combined mass, tumbling us to the floor. The big Cockney wrapped his hands around my throat and began to squeeze. "Bloody git!" he said, with a growl.

My peripheral vision dimmed immediately, turning gray at the edges as the oxygen to my brain was cut off. My hands fluttered about his face, useless appendages against his brute strength.

Harlan leapt on Charley's back, trying to pull him off, but in his weakened condition all he could do was scream. "Stop it, Charley! Stop it, Charley!"

Suddenly, he began coughing, and gasping for breath, the blood draining from his face. He was having some kind of attack, and it saved my life.

Hearing his master's distress, Charley let go of me and rushed to Harlan's side. He'd slumped to the floor, his entire body quivering, eyes rolled back up into his head. Charley massaged Harlan's throat, his face creased with fear and concern. "Breathe, Guv'nor, breathe," he said.

A pounding came at the door, jarring me further. "Mr. Astor! Are you all right? Mr. Astor?"

"Shut yer bleedin' hole, Collins! Get Dr. Medford, now."

"Right," came the reply, followed by muffled footsteps pounding down the carpeted hallway.

It seemed rather silly to be summoning a doctor for a dying man, more so to even have one on board, but with the steward gone, and Charley thus occupied, I realized nothing now prevented me from leaving.

Still trying to catch my own breath from the near strangulation I'd suffered, I staggered to my feet, using the wall behind me for support.

Charley still bent over Harlan, ministering to him, and I could see my friend's normal coloring returning,

I grasped the door handle, slipped out of the suite, and ran headlong down the hallway to my stateroom. My plan, as hazy and ill-formed as it was, was to grab my laptop and recorder, find Maddy and get us off the ship in the lifeboat Harlan had prepared for me. With two of us, the food and water would have to be conserved, and the satellite phone would be our salvation, if my laptop cellular proved inadequate, that is if Harlan was telling the truth. And assuming he was, I prayed that he'd remembered the lifeboat's number correctly.

I burst into my suite, and locked the door behind me. I knew it was an absurd gesture, as the stewards no doubt had pass keys for every lock on board. Still, it offered me a measure of comfort while I set about gathering my things. A quick look at the bedside clock showed me that it was just after five. Dawn would be breaking soon. If I wanted to get Maddy and me off the boat under the cover of darkness I had to hurry. And time would be even shorter, given that I still had to locate Maddy, and convince her to leave with me.

Going to my closet, I pulled out the carryall, leaving the rest of my clothes behind. Taking them was unnecessary and would only weigh me down. I brought it over to the bed, unzipped it and placed both my laptop and the DVD recorder into it, along with all of the disks I used for my interviews. I suddenly realized that this was precious cargo, indeed. And not just for my own gain. These were the last wills and testaments of these people.

I scanned the room one last time, looking for anything I might have missed, and I heard the pounding of feet going past my suite. That would be the doctor and the steward returning to Harlan's suite. Time was running out.

I was about to open the door, when I heard a noise coming from the other bedroom. A soft moan. I replaced my carryall on the bed and padded over to the door separating the second bedroom from the sitting area. The moan came again, soft and forlorn. Swallowing my fear, I waited, counted to three and flung it open, snapping on the lights at the same time.

Maddy bolted up in the bed, her eyes wide with fright and bleary from sleep.

"Trevor!"

I hesitated only a moment before I was in her arms.

"Oh, God, I'm so sorry, Maddy, please forgive me," I said, my words coming in sobs.

She held me, locked in her embrace, smothering me with kisses. "I'm sorry, too, Trevor. I've been so silly about all of this."

"Where have you been? I've been trying to find you for the last day."

She shook her head. "I was angry and I just wanted to be alone for awhile. So, I moved to a first class cabin on C-deck. I felt betrayed—that you'd manipulated me for your book."

"You know that's not true."

"I do now. And, Trevor...I love you, too. With all my heart."

The world shifted under me again. "You do?

She nodded, tears coming to her eyes.

"H—how'd you get in here?"

"Your man, Henry, let me in."

I nodded, trying to find a way to broach the question uppermost in my mind. I decided there was no better way than being direct.

"Maddy, why didn't you tell me?"

She glanced at me, then down at her hands. A lone tear fell onto the sheets, soaking in immediately. "You know...."

"Yes, I know. And you haven't answered my question."

"At first, I didn't think I had to tell you, Trevor. All of us know why we're here. Then, later, when Harlan told me about you, it was too late. I—I was already falling in love with you."

"And you thought I wouldn't want to get involved."

"Was I so wrong to think that?"

"No," I said, shaking my head.

And she was right. If I had known the true nature of the voyage, I not only would have kept my distance from her, but from all of those whom I'd interviewed. The whole project would have been tainted with the breath of pity. There was also a very good chance that I would not have gone at all. Still, once she'd known that I was not among the terminally ill, she owed me the truth. I should have been angry, yet I wasn't. Perhaps because the truth about her condition still hadn't sunk in.

"What are you thinking?" she asked, breaking into my thoughts.

"That you're right...*and* wrong. You should have given me the benefit of the doubt, Maddy."

"Maybe if you knew the whole story, you'd think differently." She glanced toward the other bedroom. "I assume you've got your recorder with you."

"You want me to interview you, *now?*"

"Yes."

"Maddy, we've got to get off this ship. If we don't leave soon, we might not have another chance. One of Harlan's goons just tried to kill me."

I started to rise and she grabbed my arm, surprising me with the strength of her grip. "Wait."

"Maddy, we have no time."

"Sit down, Trevor."

Her tone was adamant, and I sat back down on the bed, my anxiety level rising. "You're in no danger from Harlan, or anyone else. All of us have made our peace with God and life. Because of this, we have nothing to fear, least of all death coming sooner. Harlan loves you as he would a brother. He's forgiven you; he wants you to live."

"And what about you, Maddy. Don't you want to live?"

She shook her head. "Please, don't."

"Now, hold on a minute. You wanted to be interviewed. You have to be willing to take the hard questions."

"Okay," she said, whispering.

"I must be crazy, but if what you say about Harlan is true, and the fact that no one has busted down the door supports it, then we might as well talk, that is, if you really want to, Maddy."

"I do."

I ignored the other connotation those words conjured and went back into my room. I reached for my carryall and listened for the rush and clatter of footsteps coming down the hall, but silence continued to reign. Perhaps it was true. Perhaps my friend *had* forgiven me my anger.

Unzipping the carryall, I pulled out the DVD recorder and a blank disk and brought them back into the second bedroom. Maddy was already up and putting on her clothes. I waited until she'd finished, then pointed to the Biedermeier chairs. "Why don't we do it over here," I said.

She nodded and sat down. I seated myself on the other chair, placing the recorder on the small table between us.

"Are you ready?"

Her face split into one of her wry smiles. "As much as I'll ever be," she said.

"All right. Just state your name, age, and occupation, then go wherever you want with it. It's up to you."

She nodded and I reached for the record button.

FRIDAY

APRIL 13, 2012

15

Interview with Maddy Regehr
Location: Suite B-57/59

Now that I'm doing this, I feel so stupid, like I'm giving a deposition, or something."

"You want to stop? You don't have to do it, you know."

"No, let's go on." She fell silent for a moment, then nodded. "My name is Madeleine Regehr, I'm thirty-six years old, and I'm a burned-out interior designer." She laughed, then fell silent again, her expression turning serious. "I've often wondered how a life can go awry. Is it the paths we consciously choose for ourselves, or the roads we leave untrammeled? Is it the big things, or the little things with interest compounding daily, that finally break us? It was these kinds of questions that filled my head when I left for college. I'd lived most of my life in a small Connecticut town, swathed in the bliss that comes with the ignorance of the privileged. Don't get me wrong, the nineties hadn't passed us by. We had troubled youth, a crime index that would have shocked a big city, and a divorce rate off the scale. My own parents were anomalies—they'd been married for twenty years and were happy."

"But you weren't?"

"No. I guess it was because I felt stifled in that little town. Besides being dry, it had nothing for a young person to do, so you spent your time looking for trouble...and finding it. I was caught shoplifting—twice, prompting my parents to send me off to boarding school in the tenth grade. I fought it at first, managing to fail out the first semester. My parents drove up to the school and we spent the whole drive back in silence. Somehow, that was worse than if they'd yelled at me."

"Were you glad to be home?"

"No. About the third day I was back, I realized that it was worse than being in boarding school, that my friends had no ambitions other than to get married, live in their husband's shadows, and screw the tennis pro at the country club. I begged my Mom and Dad to send me back, promising to make straight 'A's.'

"They were skeptical, but I won them over. I think it was my father who saw it first, recognizing in me a little something of himself at that age. He convinced my Mom, and they in turn convinced the school. Apparently, it wasn't easy, as I'd been far from their ideal student. Their proviso was that I study at home and take their final exams under the watchful eye of a hired proctor.

"It was one of the hardest things I'd ever done. Throughout the entire summer, my parents and I played the roles of teachers and student, spending six, seven, sometimes eight hours a day drilling me in the finer points of high school curriculum. I think we all learned a new respect for each other.

"Anyway, two weeks before the new school year was to begin, I took the exams and aced every one of them, the lowest grade being a 'B.' My Mom and Dad were so proud, and I felt something I'd never felt before: a sense that I could do anything I wanted, that I *didn't* have to end up like my friends, as some trophy wife.

"I worked my butt off for the next two years and got those straight 'A's.' I ended up grabbing a choice scholarship to Yale, where I majored in philosophy."

"Still trying to answer those questions?" I asked.

Maddy smiled.

"I'm nothing if not stubborn. It was that and a yearning to learn more about myself and the rest of humanity, to try and make some sense of it all."

"Did you?"

"No. But I at least could see why everyone is so consumed with living the good life, why 'things' matter more than ideas. You can grasp a Rolex in your hand, you can caress a new BMW, but an idea must first be understood. And no one outside of the department seemed willing to understand the simplest thing. They wanted to be entertained."

"Bread and Circuses."

"Exactly. And it was that realization that finally turned me off of the 'Great Quest.' And while I did not descend into the morass as did my fellow students, I nevertheless became less consumed with the inner world and more consumed with the outer one."

"No boyfriends?"

"You want to hear about that, huh?" she said, grinning. "Sure, I dated, but no one serious. That came later."

"So, what came next?"

"I managed to graduate, though it was not with the honors my parents came to expect. The problem was I'd been spending most of my spare time going to New York to visit the art museums and the tiny little galleries in Soho.

"The scene was so vibrant back then, right around the turn of the Millennium. I think it was all that apocalyptic crap everyone was going through, I don't know. But I had a ball just absorbing everything. My only problem was that I had no talent to be an artist, at least the kind I wanted to be. The breakthrough came for me when I took the wrong bus one day and ended up in the design section.

"On the street level, there was storefront after storefront selling fabrics, furniture, objects d'art, you name it, all to the trade. From the second floor and up were all the architects and design firms who patronized these places.

"I was fascinated, and I think this is where my philosophical questions were finally answered, because I felt a sense of synergy at work. I knew—without a flicker of doubt—that I belonged on that street. I'd finally come home.

I spent the whole day visiting those stores and making a nuisance of myself with the questions I asked. One woman who owned an Italian furniture store was kind enough to tell it to me straight: that if I wanted success in this business, I had to go back to school. And the only one that counted was Parsons School of Design."

"What did your parents think?"

She tilted her head, considering the question. "To be honest, I don't think they were overly thrilled with the idea. I think they equated it with the bohemian lifestyle of a Soho artist, which they were deathly afraid I would become. When I told them the kind of income I could make, they changed their tune and agreed to finance me. And as I'd had a full scholarship to Yale, it was less of a burden for them.

"I applied myself the same way I had in high school and college, and graduated with honors. The day after the ceremony I received three job offers from the top design firms on the street. None of them paid very well to start, but I took the one from Halsey Design because they seemed to be the most willing to challenge me, and because they were the best of the best.

"The next two years were the most grueling I've ever spent. Most of it was spent as Rudy Danzig's gopher. He was the firm's top designer, and he ran me ragged. If Rudy needed a fabric sample, I would run out and grab it. If he needed a floor plan, I was the one who drew it. And that was one thing that always galled me. I did most of the grunt work, and Rudy took all the credit, even for those creative little touches I would come up with on my own."

"Sounds like you hated it."

"I loved every minute, because I knew I was learning what it would take to make it. My break came the day Rudy had a heart attack. He died right on the job site. The client, a real 'Nervous Nelly,' called the firm in a tizzy; and that's when I met Matt Halsey.

"Up until that time, I'd never seen him. He had his own private office on the penthouse floor and only had contact with the senior staff and the firm's top clients. To be perfectly honest, I'd conjured up images of this real prissy prima donna."

"He wasn't?"

"No. He was about as far from the stereotypical male designer as one could get. And you'd be surprised how many *aren't* gay. Anyway, the client called the firm, demanding that Matt take over the job, personally. The problem was he was already overloaded with four other major projects. That afternoon I received a summons to the penthouse.

"I was really nervous during the elevator ride up, checking and rechecking my clothes and makeup. I'd never been up to the penthouse, and it was a spectacular view. Matt's office occupied half of it, and when I was ushered into it, I was immediately struck by its cold masculinity. Lots of glass and steel. I also noticed there were no homey mementoes, no photos of the wife and smiling children.

"Matt was on the phone to the client when I walked in, and when he saw me, he stopped speaking, and I could hear the client prattling on through the earpiece. A moment later he said, 'Gotta call you back, Merv,' and hung up. When he stood, I nearly gasped. He was so tall, nearly six-foot-three, and he'd kept in shape. Yes, it's true. We girls are as looks-conscious as you guys. Anyway, he appeared to be about forty-five, and had iron-gray hair swept back into a ponytail. Most of the time I couldn't stand that look, but on him it was perfect, like some kind of Norse god.

"He came around the desk and took my hand in his, giving me a killer smile that made my knees weak. And those eyes of his, so damned blue."

"I take it you were attracted to him, then?"

Maddy nodded. "This doesn't bother you, does it?"

"No, go on."

"He led me over to a sofa covered in black lambskin and sat me down. 'Madeleine, may I call you, Madeleine?' he said. 'I'm in a bind here. That was Rudy's client and he's about ready to pull the job. You know it better than anyone and I want you to take it over.'

"I was stunned, and told him flat out I wasn't ready. He shook his head and began parroting back my résumé. I was flattered that he'd taken the time to learn my background, but that was Matt. Thorough. That was why he was the best. And the fact that he trusted me enough to take over the job was the highest compliment he could have paid."

"So, you took it over?"

"Yes. And I had it completed two weeks ahead of schedule, and under budget. The client was thrilled, and so was Matt. He started throwing me other jobs and gave me an assistant. We began dating soon after that. It just seemed like a natural extension of our working relationship.

"Six months later we became partners, and a year after that we were married. On our wedding night, Matt told me he wanted five kids. He'd come from a big family, you see. And so that became our number one priority."

"Was it a problem?"

"We didn't think it would be, at first, but after almost two years of trying, we went to a specialist. Matt got a clean bill. It seems his sperm count was more than high enough. It was me, something I had long feared. You remember my saying that I dated a lot? Well, I was also a stupid kid who never used contraception. It was a wonder I never got AIDS. I never got pregnant, either. And I thought I was just lucky."

"So, what did you do?"

"We were referred to a fertility specialist who was using a new treatment, a combination of new drugs, that sort of thing. See, the problem with most of the drugs is the risk of multiple births. We wanted those five kids, just not all at once. And this doctor's program had a high incidence of single births. After spending the night talking about it, Matt and I opted to enter the program. I was pregnant two months later.

"Well, Matt was overjoyed, and wanted me to stay at home and off my feet. I told him to go take a flying leap. Business at Halsey & Regehr had tripled and he needed me to keep things from falling apart. I was touched that he wanted to play the chivalrous husband, but we had too much at stake. I worked right up until our son was born in August, 2007. We named him Rudy, after my old boss, who'd brought us together in his unorthodox fashion.

"The trouble didn't start until four years later. You might remember all the controversy about the fertility doctor whose patients began dying of ovarian cancer?"

"He ended up committing suicide rather than face prison, didn't he?" I said.

"That's right. And I knew something was wrong for about a month before I worked up the courage to see my gynecologist. Sure enough, she found malignant tumors in both ovaries. Matt was devastated, and scared to death. He told me the night before the surgery that if anything happened he wouldn't want to live without me. I told him to shut up and think about Rudy. That he would need his daddy more than ever.

"The next morning we drove to the hospital and I hugged Matt for the longest time. A part of me was scared that I wouldn't come out of the anaesthesia. I was both relieved and terrified when I woke up in recovery. Matt and Rudy were right there, and so were Mom and Dad. He'd called them and they'd taken the train in from Wilton that morning. They were all smiling. 'What, what is it?' I said.

"'They got it all, honey,' Matt said. 'They got it all.'

"I burst into tears then, for as wonderful as that news was, it was the death knell for me as a childbearing woman. And the real hell was only beginning. I had a regimen of both radiation and chemotherapy. My hair fell out and I felt like shit most of the time. The real irony here was that Matt ended up shouldering the entire workload at the office. He was a real trooper and never once voiced or showed the slightest resentment. All he wanted was for his redheaded angel to get well. And then the bottom fell out of my world.

"Matt had been working late and he took the last train out to our house in Greenwich. The roads where we live are narrow and winding, and it was a Friday night.... He never had a chance. Some carload of kids drunk off their asses came careening down the hill leading to our house and slammed into his Porsche Boxster going fifty miles an hour. People said you could hear the crash for blocks, but I was asleep at the time, too tired from chemo and from dealing with a four-year-old to wake up." Maddy stopped speaking, tears sprouting from her eyes. "Oh, God, they wouldn't even let me see him...said he was too awful to look at. My handsome man was dead and mutilated, and I was all alone with our child, not knowing if I would ever be strong enough to go on."

"We can stop now, if you'd like."

"No, I want to tell this."

"All right."

"I don't know how I kept it together for the funeral, but Mom and Dad were terrific. They came and basically moved in with me, taking up the slack where I couldn't.

Gradually, as the days turned to weeks, I found myself feeling better physically, though there was a big hole in my heart. I threw myself into my work and it saved my sanity. Rudy was going through a bad time then, and I didn't know how to deal with it. Mom seemed to have a way with him, and I let her take over. Maybe I shouldn't have, but it was the easy way out, and things had just been too hard."

"Business was good, at least?"

"Business was great. I found that I had a knack for selling, something Matt had always done, and the clients flocked to us. I hired on more associates and immersed myself in it. Looking back, I know it was a mistake. For two reasons. I neglected my son, and the cancer came back. You see, they didn't really get all of it and what they missed bided its time, waiting for my body's defenses to weaken. This time it went into my lungs. That's why I have this scar, from the exploratory surgery. They just opened me up, took one look and closed. They told me I had maybe six months."

"When did you hear about *Titanic*?"

"I guess when the news broke, like everybody else. It brought back memories of seeing the film when I was a teenager. Did I tell you it was Matt's favorite, too?"

"No."

"He'd loved it, thought it was one of the most blatantly sentimental movies in years. Called it a 'blow against cynicism.' He was right about that.

"Anyway, when I first heard about it, I thought it was all a joke, until I saw the footage of the launching. I'd seen Harlan around town at various charity functions. You couldn't be a successful business owner and not get invited. I called his office and he graciously arranged to meet with me the next day. That's when he told me the purpose for the voyage, and asked me if I was prepared to end my life."

"And were you?"

"Yes. I had no future, and I didn't want my son to see his mother wasting away, as I surely would."

I took her hand, feeling her warm flesh against mine. It didn't seem possible that this vital woman would be taken from me.

"Harlan's way sounded romantic and dignified," she continued. "Only I didn't count on—"

"Me."

"YES!" she screamed. "Now all I can think about is wanting to live! To be with you and see my little boy again!"

Maddy doubled over, and screamed a wordless howl of pain. I snapped off the recorder and went over to her, took her in my arms, my heart breaking along with hers.

16

I don't remember how long Maddy cried, but I know that I would have held her forever. I wanted to be her Galahad, but I felt helpless and humbled in the face of all she had suffered and endured. And though my mind railed against all she had told me, I loved her all the more, for she was the most courageous woman I've ever known. After what seemed an exquisite eternity, her sobbing quieted and her breathing became slow and even. She stirred in my arms, then, lifting her head from my shoulders.

"I'm all right now," she said.

"Are you sure?"

She nodded, wiping her red-rimmed eyes.

"Did you mean what you said, Maddy?" I asked her, my apprehension rising. "Do you want to be with me...and see Rudy again?"

The green of her eyes seemed to glow in the warm amber light suffusing the suite. "More than anything. But, Trevor, I—I don't have much time."

I caressed her face, tracing her jawline with my index finger. "Maybe you don't, then again, maybe you do. Who the hell knows? The first step is *wanting* it. I can't tell you how many times I've read or heard about spontaneous remissions. A lot of it has to do with mental attitude. And they're always coming up with new treatments...."

Maddy nodded.

"I know all that, and God knows I've prayed for it.... But what if I'm not one of the lucky ones?"

I bit back the wave of emotion threatening to sweep over me, and met her penetrating gaze. "Then we'll enjoy every moment we have together. You, me, and Rudy."

She threw her arms around me then. "Jesus, you're too good to be true."

"No, I'm not. I stay up to all hours writing when I'm under a deadline, I'm crabby if I don't get my morning coffee, and I snore—loudly."

"Oh, really? And do you sit around in your underwear, too?"

"Every chance I get."

Maddy laughed, the gleam back in her eyes. "Oh, Trevor, I'm so glad you came on board." Then her expression turned serious. "What are we going to do?"

I told her about Harlan's plan to put me off in the lifeboat. "I'm sure he can spare the extra food and water, and with the satellite phone, and my laptop as a backup, we'll be rescued quickly. I'm feeling guilty, though."

"About what?"

"Come tomorrow night, you and I will getting off this boat, while everyone else...."

Maddy shook her head.

"You have to stop thinking that way. People have a right to decide their own destiny."

"Like this? I mean, it's one thing to sign a non-resuscitation form, or have your life support turned off, it's quite another to just blithely kill yourself."

"You don't know what it's like, Trevor. How can you? To know with a deadly certainty that your life will be over in a very short time. All of us live an illusion, that we're somehow immortal, that it just won't happen to us. Well it does, Trevor, it does. And any way you slice it, it isn't pretty." She stopped talking for a moment, then resumed. "I know we've known each other for a mere instant of time, but I feel I can see into your heart. You're a compassionate man, who's weighed down by both society's conventions and a genuine desire to do the right thing."

"Only here, the right thing isn't so obvious."

"It is to me."

I frowned. "What are you talking about?"

"You need to make your peace with Harlan."

Maddy was right—again.

I wanted to go back, to talk to him, but I was afraid. I was afraid to see the horrifying mask of death his face had become, and I was afraid that he had not forgiven me.

Maddy picked up the DVD recorder and held it out to me. "Take this. Your book won't be complete without his story."

Right again.

"Maybe you should be my agent, instead of Marty."

"Who's Marty?"

"A royal pain in the butt, and a good friend. Like you."

Maddy smiled. "You, too. I think that's why I love you so much. You're easy to like."

I took the recorder and grabbed an extra blank disk, then headed for the door. "I'll see you in an hour or so. We'll have breakfast. For some reason, I'm suddenly in the mood for some obscenely rich food."

"Go," she said, laughing.

Outside, in the hallway, I steeled myself and walked back to Harlan's suite. The steward guarding the door eyed me with a neutral expression, and I was almost disappointed when he stepped back from the door without protest. "He's expecting you," the steward said.

I nodded my thanks and entered the suite, closing the heavy carved door behind me with a muffled click. The sitting room was empty, and I wondered for only an instant as to where Charley had gone. I put him out of my mind, spotting the warm glow emanating from the master bedroom. I moved forward, the soft pile of the carpet giving under my feet.

At the bedroom door, I spied Harlan lying in one of the two twin beds, propped up on pillows covered with gold satin pillow cases matching the satin sheets. He gave me a weak smile. "Come on in, kiddo, I won't bite."

I moved into the room, his hollow eyes following me. The room smelled of fresh cut flowers and I saw a bouquet on the nightstand. But underneath that odor was something less palatable, a sickly, cloying smell that reeked of death.

"I see you brought your witness," he said, referring to the DVD recorder. "I guess it's time for my grilling, eh?" He laughed, bringing on a coughing jag. He pointed toward a carafe of water sitting on a silver tray across the room. I went over to it, poured him some into a crystal tumbler, then handed it to him.

"You all right?"

He nodded. "Never better, kiddo, never better."

I placed the recorder onto his nightstand, removed the disk on which I'd recorded Maddy's interview, then popped in the blank disk. "We'll do a lot better if you confine yourself to the truth, Harlan."

"You sure you want it?"

I refused to take his bait, and sat down, fixing him with a level gaze. "Are you ready?"

"You really are a goddamned taskmaster, aren't you?" He said this last statement with a smile, though I could detect a note of bitterness and fear in his voice. He'd spent his whole life being the charismatic charmer. Now, there was nothing left but the truth....

Harlan nodded toward the recorder. "Go ahead, shoot."

I pressed the button and the disk began whirling....

17

"Christ, where do I begin, anyway?"

"That's up to you."

"That's certainly the truth. Everything's always been up to me.... You remember a little while ago, when you asked me if all those fancy words I spoke at the launching was just so much bullshit? Well they didn't used to be. None of it used to be. Now, I can hardly remember when it wasn't.

"*Titanic* has always loomed large over my branch of the family. We were the black sheep, the poor relations no one liked to acknowledge. When I was little, I remember my grandfather talking about how the tragedy ruined us, about how our financial fates were sealed almost from the moment the ship sank.

"You see, my great-grandmother was Colonel Astor's *second* wife. She was barely nineteen and five months pregnant with my grandfather when they boarded the ship in Southampton. And when Colonel Astor died, she inherited income from a five million dollar trust fund and use of the mansions for life, as stipulated in his will. A great deal, except for one thing: *if she remarried, she'd lose it all*. A few years after the sinking she did exactly that, sacrificing everything, and creating a permanent rift in the family. My grandfather never forgave her, or that "bloody boat," as he put it.

"I'll tell you, Trev, from the time I was a kid, all I ever wanted to do was to put us back on top, to show the rest of the family that we measured up—that we *deserved* the Astor name and all it carried and implied. I can remember the moment it all started....

"When I was ten, I went out and spent all my allowance on a model kit of the *Titanic*, the kind that are made from balsa wood. Not these plastic pieces of crap. I was curious; you know how kids can be. You hear all this stuff about something, you want to know more about it. Anyway, it took me months to build it, which I did in the attic of our townhouse in New York. Spent all my spare time on it. Finally, with the paint barely dry, I brought it down to show my parents. It was gorgeous, and I sure was proud of myself." Harlan laughed humorlessly.

"My mother got up and left the room, and my father...he took it from me and examined it as if it were some kind of bug, then he tossed it into the fireplace, right on top of a burning log. With all that fresh glue and paint, it caught fire immediately. It all happened so damn fast. In an instant, it was gone.

"You know what my father said to me then? 'It figures a little worm like you would like that goddamned boat. That's why I know you're never going to make it in this world.'"

"What did you say to him?"

Harlan grinned. "It was one of those defining moments, kiddo, ones that we look back on either with pride or regret. I looked my old man square in the face and said, 'You should talk. All you ever do is moan about what we've lost, instead of doing something about getting it back—like Uncle Bill. Seems to me, you're the one who's not going to make it. Seems to me it's already passed you by.'

"You should see the look on your face, Trev, it's absolutely priceless. And my sainted father had the exact same look. He had no idea that a kid so young could spell it out like that, and be dead-on right. You see, as a family, we'd lost our guts, our drive. I wanted to shake him up, make him see that we had no place to go but up."

"But, it didn't work."

Harlan shook his head. "No. Things got worse. We finally had to sell the townhouse, and a few of our antiques, as well. We moved into an apartment on Sutton Place that was an eighth the size, at a rent that was ruinous. It also meant I had to stop private school and go to one of the public ones on the Upper East Side. And that was an education, believe me.

"Still, I did my best to learn all I could. I also started researching the family history. My great-grandfather was quite the real estate magnate, it seems, and for his day was one of the richest men in the world. I think only that old rascal J.P. Morgan was wealthier.

"Anyway, from about age thirteen on, I studied the market. After school I would hang out with real estate salesmen, ask them questions until they threw me out of their offices. And I soaked it all in. Did I ever tell you the time I met Trump?"

"No, when was that?"

"Oh, man, that must have been around 1987, or so. I hung around the lobby of the Trump Tower and waited until he was leaving one day. He came striding out of the elevator, wearing that trademark red tie of his, and I went up to him and said: 'Mr. Trump, you've just met the man who's going to buy you out.' You should have seen me, kiddo, this skinny seventeen-year-old wiseass telling Trump that I was going to whip his butt.

"That was the beginning. As soon as I turned eighteen, I bought my first building in one of those no-money down schemes that most of the time don't work. It was a grimy little hole-in-the-wall in a part of the city that I knew was due for gentrification.

"See, one thing I realized, even with all the knowledge I'd accumulated, is that to really succeed you've got to have the knack, you've got to be able to *feel* it. And when I saw that rundown piece of garbage, I didn't see it as it was, I saw what it would *become*. I knew in my bones that this property was the cornerstone, the linchpin to the whole block. It was a steal.

"Sure enough, six months later, I turned it around for double my money, and I was off and running. That's how I was able to go to Harvard that fall. I paid my way through all four years doing the same kinds of deals. Over and over again."

"I remember you were always reading the trades, always looking for opportunities."

"While you, Solly, and Ken were pulling your puds, I was making two million a year in pure gravy. And once I'd socked away my first ten, I decided to get into development. That's where the action really is. Besides, the one thing I always wanted to do was create things with style that would last.... I built my first building off Fifth Avenue, leveraging myself to the hilt. It was a real gamble. I stood the chance of losing it all. It's still there, by the way, looking as good as ever."

"What about *Titanic?*"

"That was something that was always with me, something that was refueled when Cameron's film came out. I remember skipping out of a board meeting to go see it for what must have been the sixth time by then. I tell you, kiddo, that man outdid himself when he made that film, pulled something magical out of himself that he was never able to repeat in quite the same way. And why the hell should he? He made the best film ever made.

"I began thinking about rebuilding the ship even back then, but I didn't have the financial resources. I knew it would cost hundreds of millions. I suppose I could have gotten investors. Hell, after my first few successes, they were lining up for anything I wanted to do. But I wanted it for myself. I wanted to do it all. It was just like having that balsa wood model back, only this time my Dad couldn't destroy it."

"But you could."

Harlan looked at me with a level stare, and for a moment I thought he would end the interview right then. Instead, he smiled. "Touché, kiddo. You're right, but that wasn't how it started. What I said back at the Harvard Club was true at the beginning. I wanted to honor my great-grandfather, the man I'd modeled myself after. I've often wondered if he and I are the same soul, you know? It's kind of a nifty thought. History coming full circle.

"Anyway, as my fortunes rose, I solidified my plans. I even bought the cruise line that blocked all the other *Titanic* projects back in the nineties, clearing the way for me to rebuild the ship in time for the centennial. For her maiden voyage I intended to invite as many descendants of the original passengers as I could find, and together we would finish what our ancestors started."

"It's a nice thought."

Harlan nodded. "Yes, it was."

"What happened, Harlan?"

"It was two years ago, right after I'd laid the keel in Gdansk that I started feeling lousy. I put it down to overwork, at first, but when days would go by and nothing changed, I went to my internist. He told me flat out that I was going to die if I didn't stop working the hours I was putting in and start chemo immediately. The construction on the ship was proceeding smoothly, and most of my other projects were under control, so I booked into a sanitarium in Switzerland, and for the next six months went through the worst hell of my life. I'd only been back for two weeks when we saw each other at the Harvard Club."

"You left the program early, didn't you?"

"Yeah.... I'd responded to the drugs, at first, but after a while when it didn't get any better, I got tired of paying all that money just to feel like shit. Then it became a matter of racing against the time I had left. I had all these projects going. Some I dropped altogether, told the people to go ahead and sue me. Others I pushed like hell to complete."

"Like the ship."

"Especially the ship. I wanted to see it completed. I wanted to walk her decks, see her sail this one time."

"When did the original purpose change?"

He looked at me a moment, then nodded.

"Sorry, didn't understand you for a second. It was about two months before the launch, and I'd already been flooded with inquiries from people wanting to book passage. I got this one letter from a young girl, maybe you've interviewed her, saying that it was her dying wish to sail on the *Titanic*. And that got me to thinking. Why not have all the passengers be those with no hope left? And there you have it."

"I'm really sorry, Harlan. I didn't get a chance to tell you that."

"You mean before or after you tried to brain me with that bottle?"

He laughed, then coughed wetly.

"I'm sorry about that, too."

"Don't be, kiddo. I should've told you the truth. But would you have come along if I had?"

"I don't think so."

"Are you glad you did?"

"To be honest, I don't know," I replied.

"Maddy?"

"Maddy." I watched for any kind of sign from him, then decided to ask the question that burned uppermost in my mind. "Was she a setup, Harlan? Was she supposed to keep me here, if I found out the truth too early?"

"You really think I would do that? Do you think I could *make* her love you?"

"I don't know what to think."

"I've only known her for a short while, Trev. She truly cares for you."

"Too bad it's all for nothing."

"Is it? I would say you're the richer for knowing her, and she for knowing you. And isn't that what it's all about?"

"Harlan Astor, the philosopher?"

Harlan laughed again, stifling a cough with the back of his hand. "When you've got the grim reaper staring you in the face, you tend to spend a lot of time pondering your life. And I'll tell you, kiddo, there's a few things I'd do differently if I had the chance to make things right."

"The way I see it, you've got nothing to feel sorry about. You've done a lot of great things. You've remade your family's fortune."

Harlan's tiny smile was fraught with irony. "Yes, but I've no one to leave it to, Trev. I spent so much time consumed by ambition, that I never bothered to find anyone to share it with." He fell silent for a moment, the emotion flushing his face a pale crimson. "Can we stop now, I'm getting tired."

"Sure, no problem."

Sadly, I reached for the stop button on the recorder....

18

What time is it?" Harlan asked.

I glanced at my watch. "Just after six."

"Will you open the curtains for me?"

I walked over and threw aside the heavy drapes covering the large rectangular windows. The sky was a riot of color, and the sun stood poised just below the horizon, though its rise would be hidden from our view by the stern of the ship. Harlan stared out at the sea, preternaturally calm in those predawn moments, his eyes bearing ineffable sadness. "It's beautiful, isn't it?"

"Yes, it is," I said.

"Captain Pierce tells me the weather tomorrow night will be much as it was a century ago. I find comfort in that."

I turned from the window, no longer able to remain silent. "Maddy's going with me."

He nodded. "I thought she might. Her little boy, now you. Two very powerful incentives." He grimaced as a pain shot through his ravaged body.

I approached the bed. "Maybe there are others teetering on the edge, like the ones who got off at Cobh. Maybe they'd like another shot at whatever they have left. You don't have to do this, either, Harlan. Disarm the bomb. Let the *Titanic* complete this voyage."

He looked up at me then, tears running down his cheeks. "I—I can't, kiddo. If I try to turn it off, it'll blow; it's sort of a fail-safe."

"Then let everybody off in the boats. With only five hundred of us on board there's more than enough room for everyone."

"They won't go."

"How do you know that? Tell them. Let them know it's okay. If they know you're going, the rest will follow."

"I can't," he said, his compressing into a tight line. "After the others left, I gave them my word that the rest of us would all go together."

My anger boiled over then. "You gave them your word? Jesus Christ! What the hell kind of a thing is that?"

Harlan pushed himself up, and I could see that it took monumental effort. "IT'S THE ONLY THING I HAVE LEFT!" He collapsed back onto the bed, coughing uncontrollably, and I went to him. I felt awful, yet I did not regret a word I'd said. "Are you all right?"

"I think, sir, that you'd better go."

I looked to the door and saw Henry standing there, immaculate in his white steward's jacket, the White Star Line burgee embroidered over his left breast. His expression was grave, and not without a touch of menace, something of which I would never have thought him capable. I turned back to Harlan who now had his eyes closed, his breathing rapid. His skin was pale to the point of translucence, and a sheen of sweat covered his skin.

"You have the power, Harlan. You're the only one who can change what's going to happen...."

Henry moved further into the room. "Mr. Hughes, if you please."

I walked out, stopping in front of Henry only a moment. "He can stop this, Henry, if he really wants to."

The older man's features softened.

"I know, Mr. Hughes. I'm just not sure I want him to."

His words shocked me, but they shouldn't have, for I knew a good many on board felt exactly the same. But maybe if Harlan let them know that he bore them no ill will, that it was okay to change their minds, some of them, however small a percentage, would join me and Maddy in that lifeboat. If that happened, I knew I would be able to leave the rest with a clear conscience.

I watched the sunrise up on the Boat Deck. The icy wind cut through my light clothes, but I didn't feel it. My mind was too preoccupied with all that I'd seen and heard since boarding in Southampton. I could hardly believe that only three days had passed. My heart told me it was far longer. Suddenly, I remembered something that Julia had said to me once: That time does not elapse for the human heart, that one moment could last a lifetime.

With Maddy, it would have to....

Right then, for the first time since Harlan had revealed the truth about her, and after hearing her heart wrenching story, the full weight of her impending mortality bore down upon me. I started to cry, the wind blowing the tears back against my ears.

"Oh, Maddy, I've just found you. I don't want to lose you!"

I saw someone turn the corner of the deck at the bow end of the starboard side, and I recognized the figure as that of Captain Pierce. He walked slowly and with what appeared to be a great deal of pain. What would make a man stick to his duty in spite of such excruciating agony? Especially when it didn't really matter? I shook my head in disbelief and frank admiration. He walked by me, sending me a smart salute, a warm glint in his gentle eyes. I nodded back and was about to offer some parting words, but stopped myself when I remembered my breakfast date with Maddy. First, however, there was something I wanted to check out.

Number Nine lifeboat lay between the third and fourth funnels on the starboard side, just forward of the Aft Grand Staircase skylight. I went there now, wanting to see if Harlan had been telling the truth. Climbing up onto one of the Welin davits, I worked loose one end of the canvas covering and peeked in.

It was hot and airless inside, smelling of must and canvas, and the heavy fabric was so thick almost no light penetrated, and only from where I'd loosened it. I couldn't see much, except for a few vague bundles and something that looked like a barrel. I breathed a sigh of relief and replaced the canvas. Harlan had spoken the truth.

Now, it was time to get word to someone about what Harlan planned to do.

Climbing down from the davit, I hurried along the deck to the Wireless Room. As I had hoped, Sammy was on duty.

"Hello, Mr. Hughes, how's the book coming along?"

"Fine, Sammy," I said, forcing a smile on my face I did not feel. "I want to send another dispatch."

Sammy's smile slid off his face.

"I'm so sorry, sir, but Mr. Astor has ordered radio silence. We can receive...but no transmissions are allowed for the duration of the voyage."

An icy finger slid up my spine. "But surely you can let me get out my last dispatch...."

"I wish I could, Mr. Hughes, but they've even taken the transmitter tubes." He pointed to one of the antique radio components and I could indeed see a couple of empty tube sockets.

I was about to protest when I remembered my laptop. With its cellular function, I wouldn't need the Marconi wireless. Feeling a little foolish, I bade Sammy a cheery good morning and headed down to my suite.

The laptop was missing from its place inside my dresser. And since the bed had been made, I knew Henry had been there. Fuming, I started out the door toward Harlan's suite, then thought better of it. They didn't want me to get a message out, that much was obvious. But what angered me was that for all of Harlan's grandiloquent words, he didn't trust me, and that hurt. And going there would only alert them that I knew.

Disgusted, I left the suite and took the Grand Staircase down to D-deck. I found Maddy at her usual table by the window. Her loving smile turned to a frown of concern when she saw the troubled look on my face. I sat down and quickly brought her up to date.

"What do you think he's going to do?" she asked when I'd finished.

"I honestly don't know, Maddy," I replied. "I thought I knew him, but obviously, I didn't."

"Maybe you need to give him the chance."

I was about to offer a reply when a steward came up bearing a bottle of champagne. "Compliments of Captain Pierce, Mr. Hughes," he said, showing me the label. It was a Dom Perignon, 2002 vintage, an exceptional year for that vintner. Unfortunately, I wasn't really in the mood for it, yet to refuse the gift would have been unthinkable. Maddy seemed to sense my reticence.

"How about a mimosa," she offered, "it'll be romantic."

I turned to the steward and nodded my assent, and he turned and left. He appeared a few moments later with two tall glasses filled with the mixture of orange juice and the Dom Perignon. I lifted my glass and turned to the captain's table, nodding my thanks. Curiously, he avoided my gaze. I turned back to Maddy.

"I guess he thinks mixing champagne with orange juice is barbaric. Anyway, here's to us."

Maddy lifted her glass, a sad smile on her face. "To us," she echoed.

I found the mimosa cold and refreshing, draining it in three swallows. The steward returned and took our food orders, and I opted for the Eggs Benedict, the lightest thing on the menu. While we waited for our breakfast, we talked of our lives prior to meeting. I spoke of my latest novel, and she her last design job. We both knew we were avoiding what was uppermost in our minds, but we needed the respite.

When the food arrived, I dived in, savoring the delicious subtleties of the Hollandaise sauce. And then I suddenly felt dizzy, overwhelmed by the fatigue I'd staved off for the entire night.

"Are you all right?" Maddy said, concerned.

"I think I need a long nap, maybe then I'll be able to make sense of everything."

"You want some company?"

She said this without a trace of coyness, and I knew she meant it to be taken at face value. And the truth was, I didn't want to be alone.

"Yes, I would."

We left the Dining Saloon and took one of the lifts up to B-deck and let ourselves into my suite. Once again, Henry had been in to straighten up. The dizziness overwhelmed me again, and I sat in one of the Biedermeier chairs, while Maddy turned down the bed. She helped me undress and into the bed, then climbed in after me.

"Sleep well, my Galahad," she said.

Her voice echoed, and my head felt as if it were swathed in cotton.

"What did you say?" I said, my tongue feeling thick and clumsy. I tried to sit up and another wave of dizziness washed over me.

"Maddy? What's happening to me?"

And I blacked out....

Saturday
April 14, 2012

19

When I awoke, darkness had fallen. I lay for a full minute trying to get my bearings. My head throbbed with a dull ache, and my mouth tasted of old pennies. Shaking my head to clear it, I sat up with a groan, trying to figure out what it was that was bothering me.

Something was different. And then it hit me.

The vibration of the ship had ceased. We'd come to a stop. I fumbled for the light switch and snapped it on, flooding the room with soft amber light. Maddy was gone.

Her side of the bed was neatly tucked in, and her clothes were no longer piled on one of the Biedermeier chairs, as it had been earlier that day. I got up and padded into the other room. That, too, was empty. It was then that I suddenly felt an overwhelming need to relieve myself and ran into the bathroom settling onto the archaic water closet just seconds before I would have had an accident. Another wave of dizziness washed over me when I stood up, and I waited until it passed before moving on.

Returning to my own bedroom, I picked up my watch. The hands read: 10:30. I'd slept for over twelve hours, not unusual when I'd stayed up half the night. And then I noticed the day/date windows: *SAT 14.*

I stood there a full minute just staring at the watch face, trying to figure out how I could have slept for over *twenty-four* hours.

I'd been drugged.

That explained why my bowels had been at the bursting point, and that was why Captain Pierce had not been able to meet my eyes. No doubt Harlan had wanted to make sure that I had no avenues left with which to thwart his desire for the ultimate *felo-de-se*.

A bitter, sulphurous anger shot through me, coupled with a profound sense of helplessness. I grabbed my clothes and pulled them on, all the while trying to formulate what to do next.

Stepping into my shoes, I went to the dresser for my belt and keys. It was there I spotted the note written on the cream-colored *R.M.S. "Titanic"* stationery, lying atop my accessories:

It's time to leave. Meet me on the Boat-Deck. Love, Maddy.

I folded the note and stuffed it into my trouser pocket. I was happy beyond measure that she was waiting for me, though I was also puzzled that she'd gone on ahead. I took one last look around my suite, my eyes coming to rest on the framed black-and-white photograph of Arthur and Emily Ryerson. I bid them a silent farewell and left.

The hallway was completely deserted and for some reason, the lifts were not operating. When I entered the foyer for the Grand Staircase, I also found it devoid of people. Where the hell was everyone?

I emerged onto the Boat Deck and immediately spotted two crewmen, Charley and the one he'd called Collins, busily preparing Lifeboat Nine. Maddy stood off to the side. And she was not alone. With her, leaning on Henry for support, was Harlan, still dressed in his red silk dressing gown, his once lustrous hair in disarray. I walked up to them, noting their grave expressions.

"What's going on, here, Maddy?" I asked.

"Time for you to go, kiddo," Harlan answered.

"I wasn't talking to you."

Maddy moved toward me, carrying my laptop inside its carry case. She handed it to me and I saw she was crying. The cold terror I felt gripping my heart had nothing to do with the chill breeze now blowing across the deck, making the steel guy wires supporting the funnels sing with a mournful moaning sound.

All else was silence.

I grabbed her by the shoulders, trying desperately not to lose control. I knew that if I did, I stood no chance of changing her mind.

"Why, Maddy? I thought we'd agreed to do this together."

She broke down then and clutched me fiercely, each one of her sobs a knife through my heart. Looking over her shoulder, I glared at Henry and Harlan. Suddenly, the ship's tri-tone whistle's blew. Three long, three short, and three long again. S.O.S.

Before I could wonder about the significance of this, my silent question was answered when I saw throngs of passengers emerging from every egress point. As with Mrs. Bates' funeral, they did not speak, moving with solemn grace. The took up positions all around us, staring mutely. I couldn't help thinking that this was indeed another funeral. But who's was it? Mine...or theirs?

No longer able to remain silent, I shouted over the wind. "Tell her it's okay to leave, Harlan! Tell them *all* it's okay."

Harlan shook his head.

"I'm sorry, Trev, but we've come too far to turn back, now. This is the only way left for us."

I looked down at Maddy. "Is this what you *really* want?"

"No," she said, shaking her head, her voice cracking. "It isn't. But last night, after you fell asleep, Henry came in and we talked. He told me that they'd drugged your champagne, that you might try something desperate, and they couldn't allow that."

"But what about what we planned, what about our future?"

Her lips trembled. "We have no future, Trevor, we never did. I guess I let myself get swept up in your optimism, and I'll always love you for giving me that one last burst of hope. But the truth is I am dying, and there's nothing anyone can do to stop it."

I started to protest and she put a finger to my lips. It felt burning hot against my skin, as if she were consuming the last of herself at that very moment.

"No, please listen. Hear me out. I love you with all my heart, Trevor. Aside from Matt and little Rudy, you're the best thing that's ever happened to me. But I can't go back.... I can't look into my little boy's eyes again and see that hope in his eyes, too, knowing it's all a lie. If I do, I'll be lost forever."

"So, that's it? You're just going to give up the fight?"

She gazed into my eyes then, her own filled with such inexpressible despair. "I've already lost it, Trevor, the battle's over."

She pressed the laptop into my hands and backed away. "No, Maddy, no!" I screamed, advancing on her. Charley and the other crewman materialized from out of the crowd and grabbed me by each arm.

I struggled, like a fish on a hook, screaming her name. Crying hysterically, she ran into the crowd, which parted to let her in, then closed around her.

"MADDY!"

"Come on, mate, let's not make this any harder," Charley said, his voice tinged with sympathy.

I shot him a smoldering glance and allowed them to move me toward the Number Nine lifeboat, which had been lowered on the davit. I could now clearly see the supplies, and noted that there were at least ten days of food and water. So, she *had* been planning to go, until....

I stopped abreast of Harlan, my eyes filled with hate. "I'll never forgive you for this," I said.

"That's okay, Trev," he said, nodding sadly. "I just hope you'll be able to forgive yourself."

I wanted to leap on him right then, tear his black heart out, but Charley, sensing I might again try something, tightened his grip. "Let's go," he said pushing me toward the boat.

Resigned to my fate, I let them help me into the lifeboat, and then Charley handed me the satellite phone.

"Remember your promise," he said, drilling me with his dark brown eyes.

"Go to Hell," I said.

He nodded, a wistful smile creasing his weathered face. "More than likely, mate, more than likely." He turned to the two crewmen manning the davits and shouted: "Lower away!"

They began turning the cranks as fast as they could. The gears creaked and groaned while I descended to the water over fifty feet below. As had been predicted, the night was calm, the sea like a sheet of obsidian. Tucked in with the food and water, I found several blankets, and I unfolded one, wrapping it around me.

When the boat hit the water, I had no choice but to undo the falls, casting me adrift. The ship's engines started up again, and from where I sat they sounded like the angry rumblings of some ancient sea god. Slowly, inexorably, the *Titanic* began moving forward, the silence split by the sound of the ship's tri-tone whistle blowing a long blast in salute.

I looked down at my hands, which still clutched the satellite phone with white-knuckled intensity. My finger hovered over the power button, and I debated whether or not to make the call then and there, promise be damned. But I knew that I wouldn't. Not because I agreed with what they were doing, but because I had given my word. I found myself recalling Harlan's words with bitter irony: *It's the only thing I have left.*

I placed the phone into my carryall, which had been placed into the boat, no doubt while I lay in a drugged stupor. All my clothes were neatly pressed and folded.

Henry. Right and proper to the last.

Such an enigmatic man, so devoted to duty, just like the captain. Two dinosaurs in a world that no longer had any room for them.

The *Titanic* was farther away now, and I noticed that all its lights were ablaze, and I could hear, very faintly, the strains of a waltz being played by the band. I glanced at my watch, and saw it was now just after eleven. In about half an hour, at precisely 11:40, the explosives would detonate, ripping open the hull and letting in the icy Atlantic— just as it did one hundred years before.

And just as it did on that cold April night so long ago, *R.M.S. Titanic* would crack in half and sink to a watery grave two and a half miles down to rest beside its rusted ancestor. Only this time, no lifeboats would be launched.

This time, there would only be *one* survivor....

Saturday
May 5, 2012

20

I clicked off the DVD recorder and sat back in my chair, regarding Solly and Ken with tired eyes and a battered soul. At their request, I had returned to the Harvard Club the next day. It was now late afternoon and the sun slanted through the front parlor's windows, making bright grid patterns on the thick red carpet. I took a sip of my wine and spoke.

"In case you were wondering, I did what Harlan asked me, what I'd promised him. I didn't use the satellite phone until dawn the next morning. In all, I spent two full days in that lifeboat before a Coast Guard helicopter, homing in on the phone's signal, found me and brought me back to their station in Portland, Maine. Except for some minor exposure, I was fine. And that was the end of it. Now you know...."

Ken and Solly were silent, as were the half dozen other members scattered about the front parlor who'd listened in. That old cliché about a pin dropping would have found a home there.

Solly exhaled a blue cloud of cigar smoke and rubbed the bridge of his nose, his eyes squeezed shut. He dropped his hand and opened his eyes, a deep sigh escaping his lungs. He looked badly disturbed by all he'd heard.

"So, that's it, then," he said, drawing out the words. "Harlan and all those people just pulled the goddamned plug. Is that what you're telling us?"

"You calling me a liar, Solly? You heard those people in their own words. They all *wanted* to die."

"And I suppose that broad you met, she wanted to die, too."

"Yes," I said, meeting his smoldering gaze.

"Well, I think it's crap. There's something you're not telling us. Harlan wouldn't do that!"

I shook my head, and began gathering up my disks. I could see this whole thing had been a waste of time. Some people, when faced with a situation of such horrific proportions, just simply refuse to acknowledge the truth of it, even when the evidence is shoved down their throats.

"Where are you going?" Solly demanded, sitting up in his chair.

"I don't know. Out of here."

"You sit down and tell me the fucking truth!"

"Come on, Solly, cool it," Ken said, touching him on the arm.

The big man shook him off. "Button it, Ken, Trevor and I are talking. Why don't you go and play businessman, or something."

Ken leapt up from his chair and delivered a roundhouse punch to Solly's chin, knocking him over backwards onto the carpet. He lay there, stunned both from the blow and Ken's unexpected reaction.

Ken stood over him, pointing a finger down into his chubby face. "This is the last goddamned time you ever put me down. Do you hear me, you fat piece of shit?"

Solly nodded dumbly, rubbing his chin.

"Good, then I want you to get up and get the hell out of here, go take Karen to a fucking show...or something."

Solly struggled to his feet, his face mottled red. He looked as if he was going to say something else, to get in the last word, as he always had to do. Then he seemed to deflate, looking for all the world like what he was: a middle-aged bully who'd finally been put in his place.

"Fuck it," he said, and stalked out of the room.

After Solly left, Ken turned to me. "I'm sorry for that, Trev."

"I'm not," I said, smiling. "I've wanted to do that for years. But I'm glad it was you."

Ken gave me a lopsided grin. "Yeah, me too."

"Can I buy you a drink?"

"Thanks, but I've got to be going. I've got a date."

"Hey, that's great! And it's about time."

"I thought so, too. I saw Marge and her boyfriend down at Fanueil Hall the other day. She looked so happy. I was angry as hell at first, wanted to wring her neck. But all of a sudden I realized she had every right to be happy. And so did I. The next day I asked out my Executive Vice President. Boy, was she surprised."

"Did she accept?"

"Yeah. And you know what she said? 'What took you so long?' Can you beat that?" Ken laughed. "You know, Trev, for what it's worth, I'm sorry, for Harlan, for Maddy, for a lot of things. Mostly for being such a spineless wimp."

"But not anymore."

"No, not anymore.... You going to be all right?" he asked.

"Yeah, I think so."

"What are you going to do?"

"I've got a book to write, and someone to see."

"Julia?"

"Yeah.... I've got a big 'I told you so' coming."

"Life's sure full of those, huh?"

"Yeah...."

I stood up and stuck out my hand. Ken knocked it aside and enveloped me in a bear hug.

"You take care, *kiddo*."

Hearing him use Harlan's pet name for me brought tears to my eyes. He clapped me on the back and left.

A few minutes later I did too, hailing a cab at the corner of Massachusetts and Commonwealth Avenues. I gave the cabby Julia's address and settled back in the lumpy seat, trying to sort out exactly what I would say to her.

My laptop started beeping halfway there.

I pulled it out of its carry case and snapped it on, waiting the thirty seconds it took to boot. As a call was coming through, my cellular software automatically loaded. The screen faded up on Jane Hurddiger, Harlan's estate attorney. She had a hopeful look on her spinsterish face.

"Ahh, Mr. Hughes, I was hoping I would catch you. I believe I may
have a buyer for the Gramercy Park properties."

"That was quick. Who is it?"

"Is that really important, Mr. Hughes?"

"Yes, it is," I said, my impatience growing. "I'm the owner and I
want to know who's buying. Is that so unreasonable?"

She shook her head. "No, I suppose not." She riffled through her
papers "The buyer is a Mr. Solomon Rubens."

I burst out laughing. Harlan was barely cold, and Solly was already
feeding on the corpse. For a fleeting moment I contemplated pulling
the properties off the market just to tweak him for all the years of crap
he'd put us through, but I decided to let it go through. One thing I
knew about Solly. Harlan had been his *only* true friend.

Jane looked confused. "I fail to see what's so funny, Mr. Hughes. Is
this buyer suitable?"

"Oh, his money's green enough, if that's what you mean."

"Fine. Then I think we should decide what to do with your
proceeds," she said, back to business.

I suppressed a smile. This woman was one tough cookie, but I
wasn't about to give her what she wanted: control over $400 million of
Harlan's assets.

"I think that's a great idea, Jane. And to tell you the truth I've been
giving that a lot of thought."

I saw her lean forward, poised like the vulture she was. "Oh, that's
wonderful, Mr. Hughes. Whatever I can do for you."

"That's good. I want you to set up an irrevocable trust in Harlan's
name for the benefit of Rudy Regehr. He's a minor child, so I will act as
trustee until he's twenty-one, then it devolves to him."

Her eyes were lowered and by the movement of her head, I could
tell she was taking notes. "How much of the money do you wish to put
into the trust?"

"All of it."

Her eyes snapped up, wide with disbelief and, much to my delight,
horror. "Are you sure that's wise, Mr. Hughes? Four hundred million
dollars is a lot of—"

I snapped my fingers. "You know, you're right. I think some of the money *should* go elsewhere. I want you to make a charitable donation of $20 million to the Titanic Historical Society. They're located in Indian Orchard, Massachusetts. I'll get you the particulars later."

Jane Hurddiger's mouth flopped open, but nothing came out. I'd rendered her speechless, at least for a delicious moment. "Uhh, are you s—sure you want to do this, Mr. Hughes?"

I'd burst her bubble, and I couldn't be happier. She would have to learn to live with one less Mercedes.

"Very," I said reaching for the computer's off switch. "We'll be in touch."

"Nice move, Mac," the Cabby said, over his shoulder, "but you gotta be nuts giving up all that dough."

I closed my laptop and put it back into its case. "You're probably right. Which makes where I'm going the perfect place."

We pulled up in front of Julia's town house fifteen minutes later. I paid the driver, giving him a better than average tip and waited while he drove off. I suddenly realized that my heart was pounding, and my throat had gone dry.

When Julia and I had last seen each other, we hadn't been very cordial, nor had I returned her myriad calls these last few days when she'd put aside her own feelings and attempted to reach out to me. She'd probably slam the door in my face. And I couldn't blame her too much.

The sun was just starting to set, and the air on the hill was breezy, but warm, smelling of the harbor. Summer would be early this year, as it had been ever since the scientists had confirmed that global warming was fact not conjecture. Oh, well, it was good for the people that sold air conditioning.

I was stalling, I knew it. Taking a deep breath, I marched up the stoop to her front door and pushed the top button on the intercom. At least a minute went by, and I began to wonder if perhaps she'd gone out. It would figure. And then I heard her voice, rendered harsh and toneless over the cheap tinny speaker. "Yes, who is it?"

"It's me...."

Silence...and then: "Trevor?"

"I'm sorry to show up like this, but—"

I was cut off by the sound of the door buzzing open and I pushed it inward, entering the cool dark foyer. The stairway wound upward for four flights and I found myself wishing she lived in more modern digs. Then again, she owned property that would never depreciate and was designated a national landmark. So, who was the real fool?

I was winded by the time I reached her floor and I paused at the top of the landing, leaning against the railing to catch my breath. Then I walked up to her door.

She must have been waiting with her eye to the peephole, for the door swung inward and there she stood, looking elegant in a gold silk blouse and earth-toned linen trousers that showed off her curves. Her feet were bare, the nails polished a deep crimson.

"Hi," she said, a shy smile on her face.

I felt a rush of warmth for her, immediately followed by a wave of guilt for Maddy. How was I ever going to tell Julia all that had happened?

"You want to come in, or do we stand here like this all night?"

I must have looked a little nonplused, for she beckoned me in with a friendly nod of her head. I noticed that she'd cut her hair, and while I always preferred long hair on women, the shoulder-length bob suited Julia, making her look both feminine and professional.

I walked into the apartment, feeling a strange sense of dislocation. The place looked the same, yet it was alien to me, as if I'd spent a lifetime away from it. I suppose, in a way, I had. Still, as the minutes passed, I began to feel more at home, taking a seat on her well-worn Italian leather couch.

"You want something to drink?" she asked, poised halfway into her tiny kitchen. "Some wine?"

"You still have that bottle I gave you for your birthday?" I asked.

"The one you said would be worth some money if I didn't drink it?"

"That's the one."

"It's in my closet."

"Get it."

She gave me an odd, questioning look, then retreated into her bedroom, returning a moment later with a bottle of a delightful little red that was bottled in 1999 in a limited run under the name Millennium.

"Do we need to let this breathe?"

"Don't bother," I said. "We'll let it grow on us."

She opened the bottle and poured two glasses, then brought them over to where I was sitting. She handed me one of the glasses, and I could see a little tremor in her hand. She was as nervous as I was.

We each took a sip of the wine, neither one of us looking at the other, or speaking for a long, tense moment. She finally broke the silence with the one question I knew she'd been dying to ask: "What happened, Trevor?"

I raised my eyes and looked at her, seeing the warmth and concern in her eyes. "Are you asking me that as a lover, a friend...or a psychologist?"

She remained silent, staring into her glass of wine.

"I'm sorry, you don't deserve that," I said, feeling guilty.

"I think maybe I do," she replied, taking a gulp of the wine. "When we were together, I never felt secure with you. Isn't that silly? I was always trying to analyze you, instead of just accepting you for who you were."

"And now?"

"And now I wish I had it to do all over again."

I nodded, running her words through my mind. "Sometimes even that doesn't work."

She frowned.

"What do you mean?"

I leaned back against the sofa, the leather hissing in protest. "It's a long story, Julia, one that will haunt me the rest of my life. I've told it once already, over the last two days. I'm not sure I can do it again. Besides, you may not like what you hear."

I saw a light dawning behind her eyes. "There *was* someone on that boat, wasn't there?"

231

"Yes."

I felt her withdraw into herself for a moment, then relax, as if reaching some inner accord. She put down her glass and rested her hand on my arm. "I want to hear it, if you want to tell it.... If it'll help you."

I smiled. Julia was one in a million.

Sitting up, I reached for my DVD recorder and placed it on the table, inserting the first disk back into it. I then pushed "Play" and sat back with my eyes closed, listening.

And as that voice poured forth from the speaker once again, I was relieved to note that it was no longer the voice of a stranger....